Gallop to the Hills

Patricia Leitch started riding when a friend persuaded
her to go on a pony trekking holiday – and by the
following summer she had her own Highland pony,
Kirsty. She wrote her first book shortly after this
and writing is now her full-time occupation, but she has
also done all sorts of different jobs, including being a riding-
school instructor, groom teacher and librarian. She lives in
Renfrewshire, Scotland, with a border collie called Meg.

Other pony books in Armada by Patricia Leitch

A Horse for the Holidays
Dream of Fair Horses
The Horse from Black Loch
Jump to the Top

'Jinny at Finmory' series

For Love of a Horse
A Devil to Ride
The Summer Riders
Night of the Red Horse
Horse in a Million
The Magic Pony

*More 'Jinny at Finmory' books will be published
in Armada*

GALLOP TO THE HILLS

Patricia Leitch

AN ARMADA ORIGINAL

Gallop to the Hills was first published in Armada in 1979 by
Fontana Paperbacks,
14 St. James's Place, London SW1A 1PS.

This impression 1982.

© Patricia Leitch 1979.

Printed in Great Britain by
Love & Malcomson Ltd., Brighton Road,
Redhill, Surrey.

CHAPTER ONE

Jinny Manders woke to the sound of rain battering against her bedroom window. She groaned to herself and turned over, still half asleep but awake enough to know from the light that it must be almost time to get up, for it was Monday, which meant school. Suddenly her alarm blasted the silence, going on and on and on until Jinny was forced to get up, pad across the cold floor and silence it.

As Jinny switched her alarm off she remembered – it wasn't any ordinary Monday. It was the Monday when Ken was going away. For a second Jinny froze into an intense, aching misery. Ken was going away and there was nothing she could do to stop him. Couldn't even say, "Please don't. Don't go. Stay," because Ken was going to Amsterdam to work with Bob Schultz, a master potter, and learn more about his craft. It was Ken's chance and Jinny knew he had to take it.

"But we won't manage without him. Things go wrong when Ken's not here," she thought miserably. "We need him at Finmory."

Jinny's bedroom was at the very top of Finmory House. One of her windows looked out over the moors to the mountains, and the window at the other end of her room opened on to the garden and, beyond that, to the black cliffs of Finmory Bay and the sea.

Jinny drew back her curtains and gazed down. The pouring rain had changed everything to a grey, washed bleakness. She opened her window, ignoring the rain, and leaned out, calling, "Shantih, Shantih."

In a field at the foot of Finmory's grounds two horse shapes were tucked into the hedge, rumps turned against the weather. At the sound of Jinny's voice, the chestnut Arab lifted her head, ears pricked through her draggled forelock, eyes glistening, and whinnied in reply.

Despite the thought of Ken's departure, Jinny's face

stretched into a grin. Nothing was too bad when Shantih was there. Always at the back of Jinny's mind there was the thought of Shantih. That the Arab belonged to her, was hers to ride and care for, made everything, no matter how black, not as bad as it might have been. At times Jinny could hardly believe that it was true.

Two years ago, Jinny's father had stopped being a probation officer in Stopton and had taken his family away from the city to live in the Highlands of Scotland in a grey stone house – Finmory House – standing in its own grounds between the mountains and the sea. The only other building for miles around was Mr. MacKenzie's farm. Ken Dawson had joined them to help Mr. Manders in the pottery he had started and grow vegetables for them all in his kitchen garden.

On the night before they had come to Finmory, Mr. Manders had taken Jinny and her younger brother, Mike, to a circus at Inverburgh. There Jinny had seen Shantih for the first time. The Arab had been billed as Yasmin the Killer Horse. Starved and beaten, she had been whipped around the ring in a rearing panic. Even now Jinny felt sick when she thought about it. So easily she might never have seen the Arab again. But now Shantih belonged to Jinny. At first she had been wild and unrideable, but after months of patient schooling Jinny was beginning to jump her.

"I'll be down in a minute," Jinny called to Shantih as she shut the window.

When Jinny had finished dressing in jeans and a sweater she ran downstairs, grabbed her anorak from the hall-stand, pulled on her wellingtons and dashed through the rain to the ponies' field.

Shantih was waiting for Jinny at the gate. Her rich chestnut coat was stained sorrel red by the rain and her white legs muddied. The other pony in the field was a black Highland on loan from Miss Tuke's trekking centre. He was thickset and stocky. Already, although it was only October, Bramble was shaggy with his winter coat and haystack mane and tail.

When Jinny opened the field gate and led Shantih up the garden to her loose box, Bramble scrunched his eyes against the driving rain, tucked himself in behind them and followed them to his stall.

Jinny tipped feeds into both troughs.

"It's not fair," she told Bramble. "Not a bit fair the way Mike's getting off with it every morning. *He* should be bringing you in instead of lying pigging it in his bed."

Bramble ignored her, crunching pony nuts, and really Jinny knew she didn't mean it.

Last year when she had been attending the village school in Glenbost, Jinny had ridden Bramble there every day and Mike had ridden the grey Punch. Now she was twelve, Jinny rode Shantih to Glenbost, leaving home an hour earlier than Mike. At Glenbost she left Shantih in a field and caught the school bus to the new comprehensive school at Inverburgh. At night she bussed back to Glenbost then rode Shantih home to Finmory.

"I suppose," Jinny had said to her brother when the summer holidays were almost over, "you'll be having Punch again."

"Why?" Mike had said. He was ten years old, with brown curly hair, dark eyes and an easy-going nature.

"Just asking."

"I thought you might have a reason," Mike had said, knowing perfectly well what Jinny wanted.

"What reason? I'm only asking."

"That's O.K. then." Mike had gone back to the book he was reading.

"Are you going to have Punch?"

"Expect so."

"I mean, do you especially want to ride Punch?"

"You mean," said Mike, "will I take Bramble so you can ride Shantih and have Bramble here. Your own way squared."

"Bramble was faster."

"He was yours."

"Well, that's what I meant. I just thought you might be wanting to have Bramble and not like to mention it because he was mine."

"That will be right," said Mike. "Go on, ask me straight."

"Please," said Jinny, "have Bramble."

9

"O.K.," said Mike. "I don't mind, but you can bring them both in in the mornings?"

"Of course I will," Jinny had agreed, delighted at the thought of having Bramble back at Finmory again.

Jinny twisted a rough straw wisp and began to take the worst of the rain out of Shantih's coat. She knew it was almost time for breakfast but she didn't want to go inside yet. That would make saying goodbye to Ken even closer.

After five minutes' hard wisping Shantih's coat was beginning to look less like a sponge.

"There," Jinny told her, "that's better. Not that there's much point when we're just going out again." She left Shantih pulling at her haynet and went back to the house.

When Jinny had managed to persuade her parents to let her ride Shantih into Glenbost it had been on the condition that Jinny left herself plenty of time in the mornings.

"If there is any of your last-minute scrambling, Shantih stays here and you can ride one of Miss Tuke's trekkers," her father had said. "I'm not having you galloping Shantih into Glenbost, it's far too dangerous."

"I utterly promise," Jinny had said. "I shall be quite different. I shall never be late."

So far she had managed to keep her word. Even on Thursdays, which were death days with double maths and double Latin, having ridden Shantih to Glenbost in the morning and knowing she would be there, waiting to be ridden home at night, made the day bearable.

"Thought you were never going to be late," Petra, Jinny's older sister, said as Jinny came dripping into the kitchen.

"Oh, don't start nagging," exclaimed Jinny, peeling off her wet anorak and shaking back her long, straight, red hair. "I am not late. This is my usual time. Anyway, how would you know when you're away all week?"

Petra was sixteen. Like Mike she had dark, curly hair and brown eyes. She was clean and smart by nature. When she left school she was going to college to train to be a music teacher. Petra went to Duniver Grammar school where she was a weekly boarder. "And I'll bet she drives them all mad practising on the flipping piano," Jinny thought.

"I know when your bus leaves Glenbost," insisted Petra.

"Don't nag me," exclaimed Jinny.

"I'm not nagging. I'm only saying you're late."

But Jinny, seeing the kitchen clock, knew this for herself and had vanished upstairs to change. When she came down Ken, Petra, her mother and father were all sitting at the table having breakfast.

"No," said Jinny before Mrs. Manders had time to ask. "I don't want an egg." And she sat down on the edge of a chair to gulp her coffee and gobble her way through enough toast and marmalade to satisfy her mother.

Ken and Mr. Manders were making stiff, going-away conversation. Ken telling Mr. Manders last-minute things about the pottery. Jinny kept her eyes on her plate, kept her mind on the thought of school. She couldn't bear to look at Ken and to know that tomorrow he would not be at Finmory. He was going to work as a pupil in the pottery in Amsterdam until March. Then he was meant to be coming back to Finmory.

"Bet he won't," Jinny thought. "Once he gets to know the people over there he'll stay. They'll be his kind of people. He won't want to come back to us."

Mr. Manders was to drive Ken into Glenbost where he would catch a bus to Inverburgh and from there the ten-thirty train to London.

"Don't go," Jinny thought wretchedly. "Stay." She drank her coffee down harder than ever, afraid that she was going to make a fool of herself and start to cry. "Kelly feels the same as I do," she thought.

Kelly was Ken's dog, a grey shaggy dog with wise marigold eyes. When Ken had hitched a lift to come to Finmory Kelly had come along too. Now he was lying by Ken's chair, nose fitted precisely between his outstretched paws, his eyes fixed on Ken's face.

Ken Dawson was eighteen. After he had been put on probation for a crime he hadn't had anything to do with, his wealthy parents had washed their hands of him and Ken had become part of the Manders family. Ken had saved Jinny's life when she had been searching for Shantih

11

in a blizzard. No Ken and she might easily have been dead. No Ken and Jinny could never have rescued Shantih by herself. Compared to Ken, Jinny thought, most people were like plasticene, changing and bending according to who they were with; their opinions depending on who they were talking to, what they were doing, who was watching them or how they were feeling. Ken was always himself. Clear in what he thought, acting not just talking. He lived on fruit, vegetables and grains, saying he didn't need to eat dead animals.

"You are going to miss your bus," said Petra, smugly waiting for the taxi that would take her to Duninver. "And don't say we didn't warn you."

Jinny had been lost in her thoughts. She looked quickly at the clock and sprang to her feet.

"I've gone," she said.

Buttoning herself into her riding mack, which was stiff and white and a special present for going to her new school, she came back to say goodbye to Ken.

"Send me some of your drawings," Ken said.

Jinny nodded and looked at Ken for the first time since she had come into the kitchen. His shoulder-length hair was strawy yellow, his skin tanned and his eyes green-hazel. He was wearing his usual jeans and sweater. No one could have told from his appearance that he was setting out for Holland.

"I hope you enjoy the pottery," said Jinny stiffly. "I'm late so I'd better rush. Goodbye." And she had swung away from Ken and was running out of the kitchen.

"Hard hat," reminded her mother.

"Got it," yelled back Jinny, slamming the door behind her.

With fumbling fingers she tacked up Shantih, hitched her school bag over her head and, leading the mare out of the stable, tightened her girth and mounted. The rain swept in wind-blown shrouds, making Shantih twist her head and crab forward. Jinny closed her legs against her sides, forcing her to trot.

"On you go, on you go," she muttered, her fingers playing with the reins, her seat tight, knowing only too well how Shantih could buck or rear when you were least expecting it.

They went down the track past Mr. MacKenzie's farm and out on to the Glenbost road. The rain was behind them now and Jinny sat down in the saddle letting Shantih canter along the rough grass verge. Normally Jinny kept Shantih to a walk or trot, knowing that cantering on the roadside encouraged runaways, but this morning she didn't care. She only wanted to feel Shantih, sure-footed and swift, galloping beneath her.

Jinny crouched forward, her school bag banging up and down on her back, her mack flapping about her and her knuckles digging into Shantih's neck.

"Faster," she cried. "Faster." She urged Shantih into a pounding gallop until she couldn't tell whether it was rain or tears streaming down her face.

Dolina Thompson, settled and solid as a dumpling, sat beside Jinny in the rattling, bone-shaking school bus.

"We'll not be for the science today," Dolina said. "But it'll not be myself that's minding. Smelly old stuff it is. Gives me the jim-jams, all those dirty things in glass bottles. And that Miss Horder with her shouting and her teeth!"

"Why won't there be science?" asked Jinny.

"That Miss Horder. Wasn't she after telling us that she was off to a conference and all her classes were to go to the Hall and do that work she gave us?"

"Did she?" said Jinny vaguely. Inverburgh school was so full of people telling her to do things that she had more or less given up trying to listen. She relied on Dolina who was sharp when it came to knowing names and times and what people had said.

"That means that there will just be arithmetic and into the Hall until the interval?"

"That's right," said Dolina.

"Then I could . . ."

"What?" asked Dolina curiously.

"Oh, nothing," said Jinny.

The arithmetic period finished at twenty to ten. Jinny, sitting close to the door, had her books into her school bag almost before the bell had finished ringing. Mr. Mont-

13

gomerie, the maths master, reminded them that they were to go to the Hall and then dismissed them.

"Will I? Won't I?" Jinny thought as she marched down the corridor, surrounded by the crashing, dashing noise of the school changing classes. But already she had made up her mind. She would.

"I'm going to the loo," she whispered to Dolina and slipped into the girls' cloakroom as she passed.

Ken's train left at half-past ten. The next lesson was English at eleven o'clock. Jinny was going to see him off. She put on her mack, left her school bag on a peg and stood behind the cloakroom door, breathing slowly. Digging her nails into the palms of her hands, she stepped back out into the corridor. No teacher's roar deafened her, no hand fell on her shoulder. She pushed open the glass swing doors, walked across the immensity of the tarmacadammed yard, past groups of men still working on the school buildings and she was free. She had escaped into the Inverburgh street.

Once clear of the school, Jinny took to her heels and ran. Her long hair flopped on her back as she dodged this way and that, avoiding people and traffic. She had one thought in her head – to see Ken again.

As she ran, memories of Ken chased through her head. The way he always understood what she meant, said the right things when he looked at her drawings and paintings, understood the heartbreak and the joy that were all mixed up together in living. Jinny saw him sitting on Shantih, gazing in awe at the osprey rising diamonded from the loch; waiting at Finmory gates to tell her that she wasn't going to have to go to Duninver school and she wouldn't have to leave Shantih; Ken forcing the starving, lame Shantih to walk over the snow-covered moors to safety, and, most vividly of all, Ken working gently in his kitchen garden, growing food for them all.

Once she reached the station she paused, staring at the pouring crush of people. Then, like a hound on a weak scent, Jinny began to trot to and fro, this way and that, searching for Ken. She was certain that he was there, knew that she would find him.

Ken was sitting on an empty railway wagon, sitting

14

very still, self-contained, a silence about him in the noise and rush of the station.

"Ken," said Jinny.

"Hi." He looked at her distantly, almost as if he didn't know her or wished she hadn't come.

"We had two free periods so I came to see you off."

"Fine," said Ken. "Come on. Time for a coffee." He got to his feet, slowly unwinding his bony length and picking up his haversack as if he was apologising to it for the disturbance.

He led the way into the station buffet, bought two cups of coffee and sat down beside Jinny.

"Right," he said, looking straight at her. "Say it."

"Say what?"

"What you want to say."

Jinny felt a lump sticking in her throat. She swallowed hard.

"I only wanted to see you off." But her lower lip trembled and she had to bite it hard. "I only . . ."

"Out with it," demanded Ken.

And it was too late. Jinny couldn't stop herself.

"Don't go," she pleaded. "We need you at Finmory. If you go you won't come back. I know you won't. Stay. Please don't go."

"You've been wanting to say that ever since you heard about Bob Schultz, ever since you knew I was going to Holland. You can't stop people, Jinny. You can't hold on to people like that."

"But we need you for the pottery. You're part of our family."

"Don't fool yourself. Your Dad will manage. He's got the brains. Now that his book has been accepted he'll be writing another one. Forget all about the pottery. He was only playing at it. It's you. You want to stop me going. But you can't. So don't try."

"You will come back though? Promise me that you'll come back?"

"No such things as promises. They're filthy things. Chains to tie you up with. I don't know what I'm going to do in the future. How can I make promises?"

Ken stood up, pushing back his chair, and strode out of

the buffet; his face vivid, his eyes hard. Jinny scuttled to catch up with him.

The London train was waiting at the platform. Ken stopped at a carriage door and turned back to Jinny.

"Look after Kelly for me," he said. "Send me a few drawings. They're better than all your words."

He lifted his outstretched hand and before Jinny had time to reply he had jumped into the train.

Abandoned, Jinny stood twisting a tail of hair between her fingers. Ken's words were still hammering in her head. Everything that he had said had been true.

Jinny waited until the train gathered itself together and set off for London. At the last possible moment Ken's head appeared, his long arm waved. He was laughing, bright with the thrill of travelling. "Take joy," he called and was swept out of sight round the curve of the track.

Jinny plodded her way back to school. No one had missed her, not even Dolina who had only thought that she had sat in a different part of the Hall. Jinny noted the fact for the future.

When Jinny got back to Glenbost that evening it was still raining. The ground was a quagmire of mud and the hills textured with the white fury of waterfalls. Shantih was standing inside her shed which she only did on the wettest days.

"He's gone," Jinny told Shantih, lifting down her tack from the tiny outhouse attached to the open shed, and although the thought of Finmory without Ken was heavy in Jinny's mind she couldn't help remembering how excited he looked when he had waved goodbye.

Shantih was impatient to get back to Finmory and Bramble. She pranced on the spot, half rearing as Jinny, hindered by her full school bag and heavy mack, pulled herself into the saddle. Then with a sudden plunge she was galloping through Glenbost, past the village shop, the cars' graveyard garage and the humped village church. Jinny's toe felt for her other stirrup. Already her reins were slimy with rain.

"Whoa, lass," Jinny murmured, struggling to bring Shantih to a trot, but loving the Arab's fire and spirit, her sensitive mouth, her smooth, effortless speed.

16

"She's a fire horse," Jinny thought. "She burns up all the rubbishy things. When I'm riding Shantih none of them matter." She clapped her horse's hard shoulder, praising her.

By the time they had almost reached Finmory Shantih had settled into a steady trot, her head bent against the driving rain. Jinny was cold and soaking, her hands numb, the brim of her hard hat a water spout.

Suddenly Shantih stopped, stood stock still, her eyes goggling into the grey mists of rain. Jinny could see nothing on the darkening stretches of moorland.

"There is absolutely nothing there," she told her horse, but Shantih insisted that there was. Her ears were sharp, almost meeting, and her nostrils wide. Jinny could feel her trembling, then she gave a high scream of fear, a sound that Jinny had never heard her make before.

"What is it?' What's wrong?" Jinny cried. Her hands had lost all contact with Shantih's mouth and the Arab's sides were wooden with fright.

Shantih reared up, high and straight. Jinny clutched at handfuls of mane, then she saw what it was that was terrifying Shantih. A grey shape was crouching in the rushes, slinking and creeping closer. Its yellow eyes fixed on them.

For a mad, panic-filled, split second, as the arid stench of her horse's fear filled her nostrils, Jinny saw the grey shape as Shantih was seeing it. As she fought to stay on her plunging horse Jinny thought, "Wolf," and felt the hair creep on the nape of her neck, a cold chill run down her spine. All her reasonable knowledge that there were no wolves left in Scotland had vanished.

Then the grey shape came leaping and wagging towards them and was Kelly.

"Idiots! Idiots!" Jinny said aloud, meaning both herself and Shantih, as Kelly jumped about them. With a last snort Shantih acknowledged the fact of Kelly, admitted she knew him well.

"He'll miss Ken too," Jinny thought as she looked down at the shaggy shape trotting beside them.

"But I'll look after you," she told Kelly. "You'll be O.K. with me."

17

Kelly lifted mournful amber eyes. He knew he had been left behind and he knew that Jinny was a poor substitute for Ken.

CHAPTER TWO

"Is that you?" Mrs. Manders called, when Jinny got in from school the next Wednesday evening.

"No. Tom Bombadil," Jinny shouted back.

"You're just too late. Miss Tuke was on the phone only minutes ago. You've to ring her back."

"Did she say what she wanted?" Jinny asked, as her mother came into the kitchen.

"No. Aren't you rather late?"

"An hour late. I had to go to detention."

"What for this time?"

"Untidy appearance. My skirt had fallen off its hook and when I changed out of my jeans this morning it looked pretty Oxfammy. Then some nit spilt their dinner down it in the lunch queue and Miss Bremmer saw me and that was that."

"Oh, Jinny," sighed her mother despairingly.

"I'll phone Miss Tuke now," said Jinny, and escaped to the hall. Sitting on the stairs, she dialled Miss Tuke's number. Kelly came to sit on the step above her, resting his chin on Jinny's shoulder, snuffing at her ear and wagging his tail.

"Hullo. Pine Trekking Centre. Miss Tuke speaking."

"Hullo," said Jinny, scratching Kelly's head with one hand and thinking that Miss Tuke's voice was just like herself, full of bounce and no nonsense. "It's Jinny here."

"Oh, good. That was quick. Now listen carefully so that I don't need to tell you twice. These phone calls cost the absolute earth."

"I'm listening," said Jinny, expecting to hear something about Bramble's shoeing.

"Last week I was at a conference for trek leaders and one of the ideas that came up was Trekking Clubs."

18

"What?" said Jinny.

"Much the same as the Riding Clubs but based on trekking centres. Weekend courses, simple competitions, winter treks, visits, films. What do you think of it?"

"Sounds super," exclaimed Jinny. "But could I come? Shantih isn't really a trekker."

"Doesn't matter in the least. First meeting Saturday to get things sorted out. How about that brother of yours? Bring him on Bramble."

"I don't think he'd be keen."

"Twelve o'clock at my place. Give you plenty of time to ride over and back again before it gets dark. You'll be there?"

"Yes, definitely."

"Fifty pence – food for yourself and your nag. See you."

And before Jinny had time to ask any questions Miss Tuke had rung off.

Mike said not likely; it was bound to be all girls and he was playing football.

Jinny's father gave her the fifty pence.

"Thanks," said Jinny, pocketing the coin. "Did you think any more about Shantih's New Zealand rug?"

"Can't you knit her one?" asked Mr. Manders.

"Couldn't possibly," said Jinny, treating her father's suggestion seriously. "It's most important that they fit perfectly and you know what my knitting is like."

"Money and more money," exclaimed Mr. Manders crossly.

"Are we very hard up?" asked Jinny. "I thought that once you sold your book we'd have plenty of money."

"So did I," agreed Mr. Manders. He had written a book about living conditions in Stopton. In September it had been accepted for publication and it was to be linked with a television documentary, but the last letter that Mr. Manders had received from his publisher had hinted that the whole project might have to be postponed until next summer. "May do one day, but not just now. Just now I could do with Ken back here to help me. My pots aren't all that unspeakable but Ken had the touch. It was his stuff that sold best."

"If you think you miss Ken, I don't know what word

you'd use for Kelly's feelings. He either sits on the front doorstep staring down the drive, or wanders the moors looking for Ken," said Mrs. Manders.

"I'll take him with me to Miss Tuke's on Saturday," promised Jinny.

"Is that a good idea?" said Mike. "You'll end up in knots like the White Knight in Alice."

"Rubbish," said Jinny scornfully. "I'll manage easily. He trots behind Shantih without any fuss."

On Saturday morning Jinny wasn't feeling so confident. She had been up since seven o'clock, cleaning her tack and grooming. Her saddle, which belonged to Sue Horton, a friend who had spent last summer camping with her family in Finmory Bay, was still a pale, new shade; while her own snaffle bridle gleamed a dark mahogany. Shantih was groomed to perfection, Her long forelock lay smoothly over her dished face, her mane was a silken fringe and her tail a glinting, slipping, red-gold fall. Her legs were a spotless white and her hard body rippled with white light in the dim stable.

"You look so beautiful," said Jinny, standing back to admire her horse. "I don't think there can be another horse as beautiful as you in the whole world."

"Right," she said, when she had put on Shantih's tack. "I've got to clean myself up, find Kelly and we're off."

"Your hair's full of straw," said Petra, when Jinny came down to the kitchen, feeling Pony clubbish in jodhpurs, hacking jacket, which had been a present at the same time as her mack, and a yellow polo-necked sweater.

"Thank you," said Jinny as she removed the tiny piece of straw from her hair. "Thank you very much. Before I was thinking smart, smart, smart, and now I'm thinking straw-in-hair, straw-in-hair, straw-in-hair. Where's Kelly?"

"Lying on the front doorstep," said her mother. "Are you quite sure you can manage him when you're riding?"

"Of course. I told you."

But Kelly wasn't keen to leave his vantage point.

"Do come on," said Jinny. "You'll enjoy it. A walk. We're going for a long walk. Come on, Kelly."

Kelly gazed at her through his shaggy hair and flopped back down on the step.

"Oh, Kelly, do come on." But the dog had stopped paying any attention to Jinny. He was staring down the drive, looking for Ken, whimpering to himself.

Jinny dragged him through to the kitchen by his collar.

"We'll need to buy him a lead," she said. "He's just lying there being unhappy."

"Are you sure . . . ?" began Mrs. Manders, but Jinny had taken Kelly out of the house.

At the stables she plaited binder twine into a rough lead and tied it to his collar.

"Now stay there until I bring Shantih out," she told him.

Kelly stayed, his mournful eyes pleading to be left alone, to be allowed to return to his doorstep.

Jinny led Shantih out, picked up his lead and mounted.

"Now," she said, "keep in beside us and don't try to run off." And Jinny set off for Miss Tuke's.

Shantih was fresh, and at first she kept jogging and popping, troubled by the grey shadow at her heels. A tractor passed them, making Shantih shy and dash forward, but when Jinny had sorted herself out she was still holding the binder twine and Kelly was still padding obediently at Shantih's heels.

When they reached the beginning of one of the forestry roads that crossed the hills to Miss Tuke's, Jinny dismounted and untied Kelly.

"Now you stay with us," she warned. "No nipping back to Finmory's."

Kelly avoided her gaze, staring past her into the distance. Jinny tried to pat him but he moved quickly out of her reach and sat down again with his back to her.

"Oh, don't be so miserable," Jinny told him. "Being like that won't make things any better."

Jinny remounted and Kelly followed reluctantly behind her. The forestry track was soft with mud and pine needles. Jinny sat down in the saddle and touched Shantih into a canter. The pines smelt of resin and fungus – a musty, tickling, decaying smell. Jinny breathed in great gulps of it as she cantered on. Shantih's stride was long and even, so smooth that Jinny hardly moved in the saddle.

One second Jinny was cantering, the next, two wood

pigeons, wings clapping, burst furiously out of the trees straight ahead of them. Shantih shied violently, throwing Jinny on to her neck, and then took off at a mad, earth-shaking gallop. Her pounding hooves spattered mud like bullets. Eyes staring from her head, her neck set hard with terror, she plunged on. Somehow Jinny struggled back into the saddle, gathered in loops of reins and tried to control her horse. But Shantih tore wildly on, her own speed filling her with fresh terror.

The gate at the end of the forestry road was shut. Jinny gritted her teeth, pulled with both her hands on one rein, fighting to turn Shantih, certain she would try and jump the gate and, going at such speed, bring herself down.

"It's too high! No! No! Stop, Shantih, stop!"

At the last possible moment Shantih stopped dead and Jinny sailed on, to crash into the gate. It took her minutes to get to her feet again. All her breath was knocked out of her body. When she did get up she had to lean against the gate, one hand clutching Shantih's reins, the other arm holding on to the top bar.

As Jinny's head cleared, she looked in dismay at her blown, mud-spattered horse.

"Oh, why did you have to do that? You idiot horse," she said aloud. "What will Miss Tuke say?"

Then Jinny remembered Kelly. She knew that he had been with them just before Shantih shied, but now he was nowhere to be seen.

"Kelly, Kelly. Good dog. Kelly come." Jinny's voice was lost in the silence of the pines.

Leading Shantih, Jinny walked back, shouting for Kelly. There was no sign of him. Nothing moved in the dense shadows between the pines, no grey shape answered Jinny's call.

She walked back to where Shantih's hoofprints changed from their regular pattern to a sudden turmoil of deep-cut marks where she had shied. Up to this point, Kelly's prints were clear in the mud but after Shantih had shied, there were no more paw prints. Looking carefully, Jinny saw that there was a double set of paw prints. One set going in the opposite direction. Kelly had turned tail and gone back to way they had come.

22

Jinny stood staring down at the prints. She knew how fast Kelly could go when he put his mind to it. There didn't seem much point in trying to catch him, and if she did ride back to Finmory to make sure he had gone home she would miss the first Club meeting.

Jinny hesitated, knowing that she had promised Ken to look after his dog while he was away.

"But he's gone back to Finmory," Jinny told herself. "He must have done. There's no point in my going back too."

She stood hesitating for a long moment, then she pulled down her stirrups, swung herself into the saddle and turned Shantih towards Miss Tuke's. Kelly would have found his own way home. He would be waiting for her on the doorstep when she got back at night.

"And what has happened to you?" Miss Tuke demanded when Jinny rode into the yard.

"She got a fright," explained Jinny.

"Mud to the gunwales," said Miss Tuke, regarding them disapprovingly. "Took a toss yourself, by the look of those jodhs."

For a moment Jinny almost expected Miss Tuke to send her to detention for untidy appearance.

"I don't know why you don't break your neck," tutted Miss Tuke. "Better give yourselves a rub down before you join us." She led the way to a loose box.

"How is our beloved Bramble?" Miss Tuke asked.

"Flourishing," said Jinny, taking off Shantih's tack.

"More sense in her right ear than that flighty idiot has in her whole body."

Jinny didn't bother to reply.

"You're the last, but we'll wait for you. Come in through the front door, straight down the hall and it's the door at the end on the right. You'll hear the noise."

When Jinny had taken the worst of the mud off Shantih, she left pulling at a haynet which Miss Tuke had provided, and went across the yard to the house. She opened the front door noisily, hoping that someone would hear her and come out to meet her, making it easier for her to walk into a room of strangers. The sight of herself in the hall mirror did nothing to build up Jinny's confidence.

"They'll all know I've been off," she thought, as she walked towards the sound of voices and knocked on the door. .

"Come in," called Miss Tuke. "We're all waiting."

Jinny opened the door and walked in. The room was obviously Miss Tuke's study. A large desk covered in piles of papers stood under one of the windows, shelves filled with horsy books covered two walls, and everywhere else – on walls, mantelpiece and table tops – were photographs of Miss Tuke's Highland ponies. Right round the room, close to the ceiling were streamers of rosettes which they had won at shows. Sitting in chairs arranged in a rough semi-circle around the coal fire were nine trekkers. Three boys, two girls and four ladies.

"Your place," said Miss Tuke, pointing to an empty canvas chair. "A bit of mud won't do that any harm. Coffee? Lemonade? Sandwiches?"

"Lemonade please," said Jinny and took a tomato sandwich. To her relief, no one seemed to be laughing at her muddy appearance.

"Now," said Miss Tuke, "let's have a general introduction. Name, riding experience, where you come from. That's the way we do it with the trekkers. Breaks the ice."

The three boys were brothers. Peter, the eldest, Jim and George Hay. They had all trekked with Miss Tuke throughout the summer and were keen to go on riding her ponies through the winter.

One of the girls, Sara Murdoch, who looked about fourteen, came from a farm close to the trekking centre and seemed to know Miss Tuke well. She had her own grey Highland called Pym. The other girl, Moira Wilson, was about the same age as Jinny and owned a bay gelding called Snuff. She said she would love to join and have horsy things to go to through the winter.

"You've a fair way to come?" cautioned Miss Tuke.

"But I've Snuff to ride. We'll manage."

The four ladies were all beginners who had trekked in the summer.

"Now, ideas?" said Miss Tuke when the introductions were over, and she looked around brightly.

24

"Lessons," said one of the ladies, "and stable management."

"A weekend trek," suggested Jim Hay.

"Could we do some show jumping?" asked Moira Wilson.

"Oh, yes," agreed Jinny, "and cross-country?"

Miss Tuke gave Jinny a look that implied that when she could stay on her horse she could think about cross-country riding, and asked the other boys what they would like to do.

"As long as I ride," said Peter, "I don't mind. Anything."

Miss Tuke reached for a handy pad and pencil.

"Would every fortnight suit?" she asked.

Everyone nodded.

"Weather permitting, of course. Now I've got something rather special lined up for next Sunday. A Club visit. Have any of you heard of Lady Gilbert?"

Jinny sat bolt upright, gulped in breath before she spoke. "You mean *the* Lady Gilbert who has the Arabs?" she gasped.

"I do," said Miss Tuke. "Thought it might appeal to you. Have you once been there before?"

"Only once been with someone who was visiting Lady Gilbert. She wouldn't let us near her horses," said Jinny, not wanting to remember. It had not been one of the happiest days in her life.*

"I can believe that," said Miss Tuke. "She never lets strangers near them, but it just so happens that my brother and Lady G's niece both breed Shetlands. I got the grapevine going and I've managed to fix up a visit for next Sunday. Get the Club off to a roaring start. Only the very honoured ever see round Lady Gilbert's stud."

"Oh, smashing," said Jinny, glowing at the prospect. "How super. I've wanted to go for ages."

"You'll see how horses used to be kept," Miss Tuke told them. "Can't be many stables nowadays who can afford to keep up the standards of Lady Gilbert's. Two o'clock sharp, next Sunday. I'll show you where it is on the map. Now does that suit?"

* *A Devil to Ride*

25

Only one of the ladies wasn't sure, but she said she would try and alter her arrangements.

"Now for the next meeting in three weeks' time. I thought we might have a little competition before the ground gets too sodden. Nothing to worry about. I'll grade you. Beginners – more of a handy trekker comp – for Jinny, Moira and Sara one or two cross-country jumps."

"And me," said Peter. "I'd like a bash at the jumps."

"And anyone else who feels like it," said Miss Tuke.

Other ideas were a carol singing trek at Christmas, the showing of cine films Miss Tuke had taken during the summer and possibly a quiz with a team from another trekking centre.

Jinny sat, hardly listening, dreaming about Lady Gilbert's Arabs. Even when she was trotting home she was still imagining what they would be like. She knew the stallion, Windfleet of Bendarroch, was a grey because she had seen his photograph on a pony calendar. "There might be other chestnuts," she told Shantih. "But not as beautiful as you."

Jinny had completely convinced herself that Kelly must have gone straight home to Finmory, and even when she left Shantih eating her feed she wasn't really worried about him. As she went into the house she checked the front doorstep and, when she saw that it was empty, Jinny only thought that he must be inside.

Petra was in the kitchen, ironing.

"Are you still falling off?" she said when she saw Jinny.

"The mud jumped up and stuck itself on me," Jinny replied. "Where's Kelly?"

"With you," said Petra.

"Well, he was," said Jinny, a cold fear clutching at her. "But he came home. He must be here by now."

"He's not. Don't tell me you've lost him."

"He *must* be here," cried Jinny. "He must. Perhaps he's with Mike." Jinny ran through to the sitting room. Her parents and Mike were there, but no Kelly.

"We haven't seen him," said her father. "Not since you took him with you this morning."

Jinny told them what had happened.

"But why didn't you go after him?" demanded Mike.

"I was sure he'd come straight home," said Jinny, not wanting to admit even to herself that she had wanted to go to Miss Tuke's, hadn't really cared what happened to Kelly.

"But you know what he's like when Ken's away," said Mike.

"I shouldn't have let you take him with you," said Mrs. Manders. "He could be anywhere by now."

"I know, I know," said Jinny wretchedly, as visions of Kelly being hit by a car and left lying by the roadside, or losing his way on the moors and never being seen again, filled her mind.

"We'll try Mr. MacKenzie's," said Mike. "He often went there with Ken."

Calling Kelly's name, Jinny and Mike hurried down to the farm.

"Not an eye have I laid on him this day," said the old farmer. "It'll be the lad he's looking for."

"If you do see him, you'll keep him?" asked Jinny. "Tie him up and I'll come for him."

"I will that, for I'd not be wanting a dog loose on the hill amongst my sheep."

"Kelly wouldn't touch your sheep!" exclaimed Jinny.

"He's a dog and there's not the dog living that wouldn't be having a chase at the sheep if the mind was on him."

"NOT KELLY," insisted Jinny, but it was a new fear to add to the others crowding in on her.

Mike went back to Finmory over the hills while Jinny went back by the shore. Their voices echoed in the silence.

"What now?" said Jinny when they were both back home. "We must go on looking. He must be somewhere near here. He wouldn't just bolt off. He knows this is his home."

The shrill ring of the phone interrupted her. Mrs. Manders answered it and Jinny knew from her mother's voice that Kelly was safe. He had been found.

"He's at the schoolhouse," Mrs. Manders told them, and Jinny collapsed on the floor with relief. "Miss Broughton was coming back from a hill walk with some of her children when she spotted him. Miles from anywhere, she says. Thought he shouldn't be wandering the hills like that and brought him home with her."

27

Mr. Manders took Jinny into Glenbost to collect Kelly. Miss Broughton was the village schoolteacher, and Jinny felt strange walking up the path to the schoolhouse when she hadn't been there for so long. "Past life," she thought. "I'll never be here again. I'm getting old. Leaving things behind me."

Kelly was lying in the kitchen. When he saw Mr. Manders and Jinny he didn't come to greet them, or lift his head from his paws, only his tail thumped a welcome.

"Oh, Kelly," cried Jinny, feeling guilty as she knelt beside him, stroking his rough coat. "You won't find Ken by running away."

At the sound of Ken's name, Kelly jumped up and ran to the door, whining to be let out, his body quivering with hope.

"Thank goodness you found him," Mr. Manders said. "He got away from Jinny."

"Well, I did think that he shouldn't be wandering the moors on his own. I expect he's missing Ken. They were always together. Never saw Ken without Kelly."

"That's the trouble," agreed Mr. Manders. "We'll need to keep an eye on him until he settles down."

Jinny took the binder twine out of her pocket and tied it on to Kelly's collar. They thanked Miss Broughton again and took Kelly out to the car. He sat in the back seat, staring out through the rear window, completely ignoring Jinny and Mr. Manders, making Jinny feel like a jailer returning a prisoner to captivity.

That night, Jinny woke from a dream of Arab horses to hear the sound of Kelly crying. It was a lost, desolate sound in the sleeping darkness of Finmory. Jinny padded on bare feet to where Kelly was lying outside Ken's bedroom door. She sat down beside the dog, scratching his chest and rubbing his neck.

"It's no use crying," she told him. "No use being miserable. You are all right with us. We'll look after you until he comes back. And he will be back, honestly he will."

Kelly's yellow eyes gazed up at Jinny from under their thatch of grey hair and Jinny knew that he didn't believe her. He wanted Ken now, not in some distant, fairytale, future time.

Jinny took Kelly back upstairs with her but he refused to come into her room, settling himself down in the doorway. She had hardly got back into bed before she heard him padding his way back downstairs and flopping down outside Ken's room again.

CHAPTER THREE

Jinny let Shantih trot on along the forestry road that led to Bendarroch Estate where Lady Gilbert lived. The wind scudded white clouds across a grey sky. Shantih was going well, arching her neck and striding out at a steady, rhythmic pace. When she was going forward like this Jinny felt as if she could have ridden her to the world's end.

"On my horse of air," Jinny said aloud, clapping Shantih's hard neck. She was excited at the thought of seeing the Arabs. In her jacket pocket was her sketch pad and pencil. Perhaps she might be able to send one of her drawings to Ken. If she managed anything worth sending.

The forestry track came out on to the road about two miles from Bendarroch. Jinny steadied Shantih to a walk. Although it was a long way to Bendarroch by road, crossing the hills by the forestry tracks made it quite a reasonable ride.

Suddenly Shantih made a wild dash forward.

"Clot," said Jinny, slowing her down. "What is it now?"

Then she heard what Shantih had heard, the drum of hooves coming along the road behind them. Minutes later a bay horse came battering round the corner, its legs going like pistons, its mouth white-lipped with froth.

"Hullo," shouted Moira Wilson. "So you're what's got him going. Went off like a tornado. I do like your Arab. Is she one of Lady Gilbert's?"

"No," said Jinny. "She was in a circus before she belonged to me."

"Shall we trot?" asked Moira breathlessly, for although Snuff had caught up with Shantih it didn't seem to have calmed him down at all. He was still pirouetting and shying at nothing.

Jinny let Shantih trot, and Snuff bounced at her side, searing the metalled road with crescented hoofmarks.

"He does get so worked up," Moira apologised.

"I know exactly how it is," said Jinny. "She is exactly the same when she feels like it."

Miss Tuke passed them in her van with Sara sitting next to her.

"Put Snuff on the inside," she called as she passed. "Keep them at a steady jog. Lighter with your hands, Moira, and sit down in that saddle."

Being on the inside helped to calm Snuff, and by the time they reached the high, wrought-iron gates of Bendarroch he had stopped behaving like a racehorse.

Miss Tuke had parked her van just outside the gates. The Mini which had brought the four ladies was tucked in behind it and, just as Jinny and Moira rode up, a car stopped and let out Peter and George.

"All here?" asked Miss Tuke.

"Jim isn't coming," said Peter.

"Then that's us. Lead your horses up the drive. Lady Gilbert may well be watching us from her battlements."

Moira and Jinny dismounted and led their horses up the immaculate, gravelled drive. It seemed quite possible that Lady Gilbert might have her spies out.

"What a place!" exclaimed Moira when Bendarroch House came into sight. "It's a castle."

Stone walls climbed up to pointed towers and battlements; leaded windows were set deep into the walls but there was no sign of anyone watching them.

"We've to take the path to the right of the house," said Miss Tuke. "This takes us round to the stable yard."

They followed the path between shrubs and flowerbeds until they came to another pair of high iron gates.

"At one time the carriages would have come out of here and round to the front of the house," said Miss Tuke, looking up at the gates.

She put her hand on the latch of the gates and was about to push them open when a young man came running across the yard towards them. He was wearing breeches,

30

leggings and lacing boots with an immaculate white coat flapping from his shoulders.

"Wait," he called. "Wait there. Mr. Jackson will be with you in a second. He'll show you where to take your horses. Her Ladyship doesn't allow other horses in the yard."

"A year in a trekking centre would shake that out of her Ladyship," muttered Miss Tuke, but they all stood where they were, waiting to be let in.

Mr. Jackson came across the yard to meet them. He walked with a groom's short-strided gait that never seems to hurry but covers the ground as quickly as most people's scurrying. He was chewed leather and bone, with black ball-bearing eyes and a tight, clipped mouth.

"Good afternoon," he said without smiling. "I have instructions from her Ladyship to show you round our stables. Would you leave your horses out here." He came through the gates and took Jinny and Moira along a path through high rhododendron bushes to a range of loose boxes built from split pine trunks.

"We use these for the deer ponies. They will be suitable for your horses."

As Jinny led Shantih into one of the boxes she felt the groom watching her horse.

"One of Gazeel's stock," he said to her, not asking a a question but stating a fact.

"I don't know how she's bred," said Jinny.

"I am telling you. They all have good hocks which is not easy to find in a pure Arab." The groom ran his hand down Shantih's quarters. "Lady Gilbert would be interested in purchasing her."

"She's not for sale," cried Jinny, shocked at such an idea. "She will never be for sale."

"When the time comes, remember," said the man.

"I'm telling you," said Jinny. "NEVER."

"When you're ready," he said, holding the box door open for her.

"Please move quietly," said Mr. Jackson when they had all reassembled at the gates. "Do not disturb the mares. They are very valuable and are not used to strangers. It is most unusual for Lady Gilbert to allow visitors. Please remember this or I shall have to ask you to leave."

"Any minute now and he'll be telling us to stop talking," Jinny whispered to Moira.

"Please," said Mr. Jackson, his bullet eyes fixed on Jinny. "No noise."

The gates into the stable yard swung open on oiled hinges and Mr. Jackson gestured them to follow him in.

The yard was an enclosed rectangle. At the far end, opposite the gates, were the stable buildings – tack room, feed house and hay shed. Down the two sides were rows of loose boxes, an extension over their roof made a covered walkway in front of the boxes. The whole place was immaculate. Brass taps by the water troughs sparkled in the grey light, woodwork and paint were perfect. There wasn't a wisp of hay or a scrap of straw or a trace of horse droppings to be seen in the whole yard. Jinny gazed in disbelief.

At the sound of their footsteps, heads began to appear over half doors. Arab heads – huge-eyed, delicate-skinned, with manes and forelocks heavy tassles of silk. Jinny drew in her breath in delight. She stood for a second in a dazed dream. Her hand felt in her jacket pocket for her sketch pad and pencil, as Mr. Jackson began to show them round.

Above each box there was a brass plate giving the horse's name, date of birth and breeding. When their doors were opened the horses moved calmly to the back of their boxes and stood regarding the intruders with a gentle reserve. Jinny's eyes drank them in. Her pencil skimmed over the paper, catching in a few sure lines the arch of their necks, the curve of dished, imperious faces, and the brittle, delicate strength of their legs and hooves, and the massed power in their shoulders and quarters. Some of the mares were round-bellied, carrying foals, one had a foal peering goggle-eyed from behind his mother and two had older, bolder youngsters with them.

"All mares?" asked Miss Tuke.

"Except for the stallion."

"Who rides them?" asked one of the ladies.

"Only Mr. Ralph," said Mr. Jackson in a stating the obvious voice.

Most of the mares were greys – varying from the dark, steel grey of the younger mares to one old mare who was pure white except for the smudges of blue-violet skin at her muzzle and eyes.

"She's twenty-seven years old," Mr. Jackson told them.

"A fair age," agreed Miss Tuke. "I had one old man of thirty-two."

"Not as old as Sweet Few," said Mr. Jackson. "She was thirty-eight when we buried her."

"Buried?" exclaimed Miss Tuke.

"Her Ladyship would not permit any other end for her favourites."

By the time Mr. Jackson had taken them round all the boxes Jinny had begun to feel as if she was moving in a dream world. The whole stud had an unreal quality about it. No clank of buckets or sweep of brush. No upraised voices shouting at the horses. Only a mellow, enclosed silence with each mare more beautiful than the last.

"And now," stated Mr. Jackson, "Windfleet of Bendarroch."

He led them along a narrow passage at the side of the stable buildings which took them to a smaller yard. There were only three boxes in the yard. Two were empty; in the middle one stood Windfleet of Bendarroch.

From the gloom of his box the stallion watched them. His steel grey, dappled coat seemed rimmed with white light, the same light that struck from his pool-dark eyes. He was power and energy smouldering in the shadowed box. He brought back to Jinny the nightmares that had haunted her through the summer holidays. The Red Horse of her dreams and the Arab stallion worshipped the same gods. Gazing at him, Jinny realised how the whole yard orbited around the stallion – the mares and the men – all the labour which went into keeping the yard in its perfection was performed for the glory of this being.

Jinny stepped back from the box, letting the others in. She trod on someone's foot, said, "Sorry," without looking round and began to draw the stallion; the hard, vital mass so different to the mares. Twice, three times she flicked over the pages of her sketch pad. She hadn't caught him, there was something not right. Then on her fourth attempt she had him. Windfleet of Bendarroch stared defiantly back at her from the page.

33

A man's hand reached over Jinny's shoulder, trying to take the sketch pad from her.

"Here," she said indignantly, snatching it out of his reach. "What do you think you're doing?"

She turned to see a youngish man standing behind her. He was tall, with hunched shoulders that made his head and neck reach forward like a vulture's. He had thin brown hair brushed straight back from a low forehead. His mouth was lipless, a straight slit in his face. His long nose was sharp and his cheeks flat as if they were sucked in against his teeth.

His eyes stared down at Jinny and she shivered violently. Never before had she seen such cold, emotionless eyes. They seemed to have no light in them, no feeling. "As if he could watch anything, no matter how horrible and not care," Jinny thought.

"Awfully sorry," he said in a flat, colourless voice. "Didn't mean to give you a shock. I'd rather like to see your sketch book." He held out his hand again, expecting Jinny to give it to him.

Jinny put her pad firmly behind her back. She had no idea who the man was. He seemed to have sprung up from nowhere. But she was quite sure that she didn't trust him.

"I don't show people my drawings," she stated. "And I don't even know who you are."

"Neither you do. I'm Ralph Gilbert." He held out his hand to Jinny who shook it warily, thinking it was more like a long taloned, fleshless claw than a human hand. "Of course you must show your drawings to people. They looked rather good to me. Come on, let me see them."

Almost against her will, as if he had hypnotised her, Jinny held out her sketch pad where Ralph Gilbert could see it and leafed back through her drawings of the Arabs. When she reached the last of them she shut the pad and pushed it back into her pocket.

"That's all," she said shortly.

"Who taught you?" asked Ralph Gilbert.

"No one," said Jinny, avoiding the fixed stare of his pale eyes as she had avoided his grabbing hand. She wanted to add, "And it's none of your business either."

"You're a natural, then," he said. "They are very, very good. Looking at them I know exactly which mares you've drawn. May I see them again?"

"No," said Jinny.

Ralph Gilbert didn't argue. He turned, asking who was Miss Tuke and telling her that his mother had arranged for them to have a cup of tea after they had seen round the stables. Miss Tuke told him what a jolly good time they were all having and how frightfully grateful they were to Lady Gilbert.

"Come round to the side door when you're ready," Ralph Gilbert said and left them, walking out of the yard with a long loping step.

Mr. Jackson took them round the tack room, where the walls were hung with harness and breaking tackle.

"We break our own youngsters before we sell them," Mr. Jackson told them and he went on to outline the methods he used to break in the Arabs. Jinny hardly heard what he was saying. She was still storming inside, furious over Ralph Gilbert's patronizing manner.

When they had seen everything they thanked Mr. Jackson, and one of the stable boys took them back to Bendarroch House.

Before the iron gates clanged shut Jinny had one last glimpse of the stable yard – enclosed and dreaming; the mares' gentle necks and delicate heads blooming over half doors, like lilacs, thought Jinny, as they watched the intruders leaving.

They had afternoon tea in a light chintzy room, not in the least like the rooms that Jinny remembered from her previous visit to Bendarroch, and Miss Tuke told them about the competition she had arranged for a week on Sunday.

"No one need worry," she assured them. "The course will be graded to suit all abilities."

"Even the word 'course' is beyond my ability," said one of the ladies.

"You Four Musketeers," said Miss Tuke, "may use the word trek. You four may trek in a handy pony way. For Peter, Sara, Moira and Jinny I shall have a few cross-country jumps. Be prepared."

35

They were all standing up to go when Ralph Gilbert joined them again.

"Do thank Lady Gilbert," said Miss Tuke, beaming at him.

"Not at all," said Ralph Gilbert, almost ignoring her.

"Well, we're off now," said Miss Tuke and began to usher her Trekking Club members towards the door.

"What is your name?" Ralph Gilbert demanded, putting his hand on Jinny's shoulder.

Jinny wrenched herself free. "Jennifer Manders," she muttered.

"Well, Jennifer, could you spare a minute to speak to Lady Gilbert?"

Jinny didn't want to go. She couldn't think why Lady Gilbert should want to see her.

"She won't keep you."

"After they've been so kind to us," Miss Tuke tutted, and pushed Jinny towards Ralph Gilbert. "We won't wait for you, but see you for the comp."

Almost before she realised what was happening, Jinny was following Ralph Gilbert along a high, dark corridor hung with portraits painted in oils. then through a room filled with antique furniture arranged round a vast empty fireplace, up a flight of stairs and along another corridor until Ralph Gilbert stopped and tapped on a door.

"Come in," called a high, rusty voice and Ralph Gilbert opened the door.

"Here she is,' 'he said, pushing Jinny into the room.

Lady Gilbert fixed Jinny with a gimlet eye. She was stiff and upright, perched on her high-backed chair like an elderly eagle. She obviously did not remember Jinny.

"My son tells me you sketch a little," she said. "Let me see your efforts."

Jinny wanted to tell the old woman that her drawings had nothing to do with the Gilberts.

"Come, don't be timid," said Lady Gilbert.

Ralph Gilbert took a step closer to Jinny and suddenly Jinny felt trapped, as if the mother and son had spread a web to catch her, as if they had her in their power. Goose over her grave she shuddered. These weren't ordinary people. Everything she had seen that afternoon belonged to them – the vast castle of Bendarroch, all its lands and all the beauty of the Arab horses, all belonged to Lady Gilbert and her son. Here in their stronghold they could do anything, were in complete control.

Jinny tugged the sketch pad out of her pocket. With fumbling haste she opened it at the first of her drawings of the Arabs and handed it to Lady Gilbert. Ralph Gilbert had crossed the room to stand behind his mother and as she turned the pages they both named the horses that Jinny had sketched.

A fat, smelly spaniel crawled from beneath Lady Gilbert's chair to wag and squeak round Jinny's legs. The moment had passed. It was an ordinary room again.

"Quite remarkable," said Ralph Gilbert in his cold, slimy voice. "Don't you think we should?"

Lady Gilbert was leafing back through the sketch pad looking at Jinny's other drawings and watercolours.

"You have a gift," she said at last, making Jinny feel that if she did have a gift Lady Gilbert herself had probably bestowed it on her. "I would like you to come back and paint portraits of six of my horses."

Jinny thought of lessons and homework, of schooling Shantih for Miss Tuke's cross-country; thought that she wouldn't have time but knew that these were excuses to cover up the real reasons. There was something strange about Bendarroch. For centuries a powerful family had lived here. A family who had always been able to have exactly what it wanted because it was rich enough to pay for it. Jinny didn't like Bendarroch. She wanted to get away from it and never come back.

She opened her mouth to say she was sorry but she didn't have the time just now, that maybe next summer . . .

"I will pay twenty-five pounds for each portrait."

"Twenty-five pounds," Jinny echoed incredulously. It would be more than enough to buy a New Zealand rug for Shantih.

"Come next Sunday. Do you have paper and paints?"

"Not really," said Jinny.

Lady Gilbert got stiffly to her feet, crossed over to a bureau drawer and took six five-pound notes out of it.

"Buy the best," she said, giving the money to Jinny. "Be here at ten. Go straight to the stables. Jackson will be expecting you."

Ralph Gilbert let Jinny out of the main door.

"We will see you again," he said, looking down intently at Jinny with his ice-cold eyes. "You can find your way back to your pony? Jackson said it is in one of the pine boxes."

"Arab," corrected Jinny. "Yes, I can find her. Goodbye." As she walked away Jinny was conscious of the pale eyes following her. She broke into a run and didn't stop until she was out of sight round the corner of the house.

"Twenty-five pounds for each picture," Jinny thought and calculated the incredible sum of one hundred and fifty pounds for six paintings. She didn't think about how often she would have to come back to Bendarroch if she was going to paint six pictures.

At the stable gates Jinny stopped and stared about her. There were two paths leading through the rhododendrons. She was nearly certain that the boxes where they had left Shantih and Snuff were along the path that went to the right.

"Well, if it isn't that one I can come back and go down the other path," Jinny thought. "There's no point in standing here. No one's going to come and tell me where to go."

She set off along the path to the right. Although it was only about four o'clock, the late October afternoon was already settling into evening. The sky was a leaden grey; a chill wind whistled through the rhododendron bushes, rattling their brittle leaves against each other and making their shadowed depths dance and shape-change as the branches moved. Jinny shivered and hurried on. The rhododendrons seemed to be growing thicker and closer, closing Jinny into a dark tunnel.

Just as she was about to turn back, having decided that this must definitely be the wrong path, Jinny heard a strange sound. She stopped to listen, her ears straining, the skin on the back of her neck creeping. She heard the noise again – a low, melancholy, blood-curdling wail. It rose and throbbed and faded, only to lift again in another wave of sound.

"Hounds," thought Jinny. "Lady Gilbert must have her own pack." Yet she couldn't quite believe that it was dogs that were making the noise.

Jinny was certain now that she was on the wrong path. The box where she had left Shantih had not been as far away as this. Yet she walked on, curiosity urging her to find out what animals were making the noise.

The howling grew louder as Jinny went on. Suddenly the path gave a sharp turn and she found herself facing a high brick wall. The top of the wall was crowned with metal spikes and broken glass set in cement. It was obviously much more modern than Bendarroch House and looked to Jinny as if it had only been built a few years ago. The howling was coming from the other side of the wall.

Jinny stood baffled, then she saw that the path went on down the side of the wall. For a second she hesitated. There was something grim and forbidding about the high, blank wall, a sense of dark things hidden behind it. Jinny had the feeling that the Gilberts would not be at all pleased to find her snooping around their property, but she had to find out what animals were making the melancholy howling that echoed in her ears.

Jinny followed the path along the side of the wall until she came to a wooden door in the brickwork. Cautiously she turned the handle and eased the door open inch by inch. Stepping through it she found herself standing in front of a huge, wire-mesh enclosure. At the far side of the enclosure were other single-storey brick buildings with barred windows, but Jinny had no time to take in any details for in the enclosure were six wolves.

Not for one second did Jinny think of them as dogs. Their broad skulls, pale eyes, low-slung, heavy bodies and the thick ruffs of hair round their necks all cried wolf. When they they saw Jinny they began to leap up against the wire netting, jaws wide and slavering, thick lips peeled back from dagger teeth.

Jinny turned and fled. Her heart thumping in her throat, she tore back along the path, stumbling and tripping in her haste. She raced down the other path and in no time saw the boxes with Shantih's familiar head looking out anxiously over the half door.

Jinny tugged the bolt open, pulled up Shantih's girth and dragged down her stirrups. Out of the box, she sprang up into the saddle and sent Shantih on at a raking trot. Past the stables they went and on down the drive. At the gates Jinny dismounted, pulled them open and urged Shantih through. She clanged them shut, threw herself back into the saddle and rode for home.

CHAPTER FOUR

When Jinny told her family they did not believe her.

"For goodness sake," said her mother quite sharply, "when are you going to grow up and learn to control your imagination?"

"It was not," said Jinny, "my imagination. They were wolves. Six of them. I saw them. No one could have thought they were dogs."

"Perhaps it's a kind of safari park," suggested Mike.

"Then we'd have seen it advertised," said Petra, "and we haven't."

"Maybe he's just starting it," said Jinny. "Sort of getting the animals together. Though that lot seemed too fierce for any safari park."

"They only jumped at you because they were expecting to be fed," said Petra, who had thought of this explanation instantly.

"And I was going to be their dinner," said Jinny.

"When you go back next week ask someone about them," said her father.

"Don't think there is anyone I could ask," said Jinny doubtfully, imagining herself going up to Ralph Gilbert and saying, "Did you know that you've got wolves at the bottom of your garden?"

"You'll find that they're some kind of dog," insisted Mrs. Manders. "You wait and see."

Jinny arrived at Bendarroch at half-past ten the next Saturday morning. She had meant to be earlier but they had been cutting down trees in one part of the forestry and it had taken her nearly half an hour to force Shantih past the whine of the saw and the crash of toppling pines.

In her school bag there was her sketching pad, twelve sheets of watercolour paper – thick and porous, the kind that Jinny had never been able to afford before; a new box of water colours; six new brushes; an empty jam jar for water; one of her mother's dusters; several old newspapers and food for herself and Shantih.

Jinny dismounted outside Bendarroch and led Shantih up the drive and round the side of the house. She felt like a spy crossing enemy territory; every bit of her was tense, waiting for someone to pounce.

At the stables she stopped and peered through the gates into the yard. It was just the same as it had been last Sunday, as immaculate as a stable yard in a toy farm, brushed and scrubbed and spotless. Jinny coughed noisily, hoping that someone would appear and tell her what to do next.

A boy wearing gaiters and a white coat came out of the tack room.

"Hi," Jinny shouted. "Shall I come in?"

"Are you the artist?" the boy shouted back.

"I suppose so," said Jinny.

"Hang on then."

The boy went back into the tack room. He came out carrying a full haynet and crossed the yard to Jinny.

"You've to come with me," he said and took Jinny to the boxes where Shantih had been left last Sunday.

"Leave your horse here," said the boy, tying up the haynet. "Mr. Jackson has one ready for you to paint."

"Thanks," said Jinny, taking off Shantih's tack and leaving it in a small shed next to the boxes. "Wait there," she told Shantih. "I'll be back soon."

As they walked back to the stable yard, Jinny was listening for any sound of the wolves. She thought about asking the boy if he knew anything about them.

"It's a huge estate," Jinny said, thinking that she might

41

be able to work her way round to the subject of the wolves.

"Vast," agreed the boy.

"You know the other path," said Jinny. "The one through the rhododendrons to the right of this one. Where does it lead?"

"I wouldn't know," said the boy. "More than my job's worth to go prowling about. We're all told that when we're taken on. I've never been anywhere except the yard and the paddocks and in and out the back lane. None of us have. Even Mr. Jackson doesn't go wandering about."

"How strange," said Jinny, realising that she wasn't going to find out anything from the boy.

He took her to a large loose box. A grey Arab, white with age, was standing at the back of the box pulling at a haynet.

"Mr. Jackson says you've to paint this one first. She's sixteen. Sirocco of Bendarroch is her fancy name but we call her Rocky. Gentle as a baby. You needn't be scared of this one."

"I'm not scared of any of them," Jinny told him scornfully.

"Keep your wig on," said the boy. "When will you want the next?"

"I don't know," said Jinny. "Depends when I finish this one."

"I'll look in before lunch," said the boy and went away, leaving Jinny with the horse.

Rocky was pure white except for dove grey patches at her eyes and muzzle and straying black hairs about her eyes. Jinny went over and spoke to her, rubbing her hands over the smooth neck and shoulders, praising her, telling her that she was going to be painted. Jinny stayed with her for a long time, feeling her warm, hay-scented breath; smelling the Arab pungency; getting to know the bulk of the horse, so different to Shantih, being older and slacker.

Then Jinny took out her sketch pad and made several quick pencil sketches. She went back to the box door, took out her paints and paper, filled her jam jar from the water bucket and, crouching down on the stable floor, began to paint. She did one full side view of Rocky and one portrait of her head, half turned, watching Jinny.

When she had finished she flopped down on the straw, exhausted.

"You asleep?" demanded a voice, startling Jinny into sudden life.

"Course not," she told the boy, jumping to her feet and brushing straws from her hair.

"You were so," said the boy, laughing. "Haven't you done any painting yet?"

But Jinny wasn't listening. She took the two water-colours and propped them up on the manger, stepped back and looked at them. They were O.K. especially the head.

"That's good," said the boy. "You've fairly got old Rocky. Just the way she looks, knowing it all."

As always, Jinny hated anyone seeing her paintings and saying anything about them. Their words hurt her. She took the pictures down and wrapped them up carefully in newspaper.

"Is that you finished with Rocky, then? I've to take her back to her box and bring you Hara. We go home now until three but I'll put Hara in for you and you can paint her when you're ready."

When the boy had changed over the horses and settled Hara, a bright chestnut mare, he left Jinny alone. She heard the doors of the tack room being locked and looked out of the box to see Mr. Jackson and four lads walking out of the yard. As Mr. Jackson passed he gave Jinny a gruff good morning.

"Not the friendliest," thought Jinny, not caring.

When they had gone, Jinny took her paintings out of their wrappings and had another look at them. They were good. She felt fizzy with excitement, as if she had been jumping Shantih over five-foot walls. It wasn't that she was pleased with herself in a conceited way but pleased because the paintings were there now and a few hours ago they hadn't existed. She had used the palest greys, mauves and blues to paint the white Rocky, sweeping in the back-ground violet black, so that the Arab shone pure white. Jinny wondered what Ken would have thought of it. The thought was in her mind before she could stop it.

Instantly she jumped up. "I'll go and see Shantih," she

decided. Ken had gone. He had wanted to go. There was no point in thinking any more about it.

Jinny put her paintings safely back in her school bag, tidied up her paints, left all her things neatly outside the loose box, then, taking her own sandwiches and the feed of nuts and oats for Shantih, she set off to find her horse.

Shantih whinnied with pleasure as Jinny approached.

"Oh, horse," exclaimed Jinny. "Are you very bored?"

Shantih pushed at Jinny with her head then swung away from her, dragging her feet through the peat moss bedding. Jinny checked that she still had water and then tipped her feed into the manger.

"I'll only paint one more Arab," she promised Shantih, "and I'll be as quick as I can. We wouldn't be here if it wasn't for you. I'm only doing this so that I can buy you a New Zealand rug."

Shantih gloomed, kicking peevishly with a hindleg while she ate her feed.

Jinny finished her sandwiches and left her. "I'll go and get on," she said. "Then when they come back at three we'll be ready to go."

Jinny reached the end of the path. In front of her were the gates to the stable yard, to her left the path that led down to the high brick wall. There was no one about. Not a sound broke the silence.

"If I saw them again I could be quite sure that they aren't dogs," Jinny reasoned with herself, knowing perfectly well that she had no business to go down the other path; knowing that if Lady Gilbert didn't allow Mr. Jackson to wander about the grounds she would not be pleased to find Jinny anywhere else except in the stable yard.

"I've got to find out and it's not as if I'm going to do any harm."

But still Jinny stood, undecided.

"You're afraid," taunted the voice in Jinny's head. "That's why you won't go."

"Am not," replied Jinny and set off at a trot along the path towards the wolves.

She walked smartly, not looking to left or right, going briskly straight ahead, as if she were going to post a letter and had just enough time to catch the last post.

She came out from between the bushes, peering around in case there should be anyone about. But there was no sign of life, only the blank, unexpected wall.

Jinny hurried along the side of the wall, turned the door handle, half expecting to find the door locked, but to her satisfaction it swung open and she slipped through.

"I am right," she thought. "They are wolves."

The wolves were lying on the ground, half asleep. Two of them lifted gaunt heads to stare at Jinny through pale eyes.

"Eyes like Ralph Gilbert's," Jinny thought and shivered, clutching her arms round her body.

One wolf got up, stretched, and came slowly towards the wire. He stood considering Jinny and then went back to lie down again.

"As usual Petra was right," Jinny thought. "Last time they thought I was bringing them food, that's why they were so wild."

Nevertheless they were wild, uncanny beasts and most certainly they were not what Jinny would have expected to find in Bendarroch's grounds. She stood fascinated, wanting to get back to the safety of the stables, yet not wanting to leave the wolves. They were so different, so truly wild.

Suddenly a door in one of the buildings opened, a man came out and stood looking around. Jinny froze. Any second he must see her standing where she had no right to be. "Quickly, get back through the door," Jinny's mind flashed. "Get out of sight. Quickly! Quickly!" But it was too late. The man had seen her.

He gave a shout and came running down the side of the enclosure, yelling at Jinny. He was powerfully built with black curly hair and a yellowish complexion. And to Jinny's total amazement he was carrying a gun over his shoulder.

"What are you doing here?" he demanded.

Jinny was as incapable of speech as she had been of movement. Her tongue was glued to the roof of her mouth.

"This is private property. You are trespassing on Lady Gilbert's land." The man laid a huge hand on Jinny's shoulder and swung her roughly away from the enclosure. "What are you doing down here?"

"Don't," cried Jinny, struggling to free herself. "Leave me alone."

"No one is allowed in here." He pushed Jinny through the door and began to frogmarch her back up the path.

"I'm Lady Gilbert's guest," shouted Jinny. "She knows I'm here. She asked me to come."

"She did not ask you to come prowling about like a thief. No one comes near our kennels. No one. Mr. Gilbert has important work to do. He does not allow anyone to disturb him."

"I was only going for a walk I'm painting Lady Gilbert's Arabs. I wasn't doing any harm."

The man let go of Jinny. "Then get back to the stables if you are to do with the horses," he said. "And stay there."

The man walked behind Jinny, hurrying her on if he thought she was going too slowly. He opened the stable gates and pushed her through them.

"Stay there," he warned, "until we see what Lady Gilbert has to say about this."

The Arab mares watched as Jinny crossed the yard, picked up her painting things and went into the loose box out of sight of the man who waited at the gates.

Jinny sat down on the floor of the box, ignoring the chestnut Hara who came poking inquisitively at her with her velvet muzzle.

"Blimey," she thought, "what a place. He could have shot me." Newspaper headlines and telly news items flickered through Jinny's head. "But at least I know now. They are wolves."

Jinny sorted out her paints and paper, spoke to the chestnut mare and began to sketch her, but the pencil drawings wouldn't come right. Jinny could think of nothing but the wolves, of the gun the man had carried and of what he would say to Lady Gilbert.

Surrounded by useless, rubbishy drawings on pages torn from her sketch pad, Jinny heard the grooms coming back to the yard and the sound of buckets being filled as they set about their afternoon's work.

"Come out here, girl," said Lady Gilbert's voice.

"Here goes," thought Jinny, and not even bothering to collect her drawings, she went out into the yard.

Lady Gilbert and the man were standing there.

"Is it true?" asked Lady Gilbert.

"Is what true?" said Jinny.

"You know what I am speaking about. Mr. Paton who is in charge of my son's animals tells me that he found you wandering about where you had no right to go. Is this so?"

"I was only . . ." began Jinny.

"Answer my question," commanded Lady Gilbert, banging her stick on the concrete. "Were you near the animals?"

"Yes, but . . ."

"Then go. Leave at once. I did not expect my trust in you to be abused in this manner. Paton will see you off my land. Do not come back. If you are found on my estate again you will be handed over to the police."

"I wasn't doing anything," Jinny cried, but Lady Gilbert had turned away. Her head erect, claw hand gripping the carved knob of her walking stick, she was making her slow, stately way to the stable gates.

"Come along now," said Mr. Paton. "Clear up that mess and be off with you."

Furiously, Jinny grabbed up her paints, paper and brushes and left them at the door of the loose box.

"Those belong to Lady Gilbert," she said. "I'll leave them there."

But she did not leave her two paintings of the white mare.

From the tack room Mr. Jackson watched them cross the yard, prisoner and policeman. Mild heads turned, gazing from foal dreams, as the gates were shut behind Jinny.

"I think you are all completely daft," declared Jinny as she was marched off to collect Shantih. "First she asks me to come here and paint her horses. I ride all this way and now she tells me to go. I wasn't doing anything. I was only having a little walk after my lunch. Nutters if you ask me."

Mr. Paton was deaf to Jinny's protests. He watched

silently while Jinny tacked Shantih up and mounted. Then he tried to lead Jinny up the path.

"No way," thought Jinny, making Shantih plunge suddenly forward, tossing Mr. Paton off into the bushes.

She didn't stop trotting until she reached the gates of the estate. As she was closing them from outside, Mr. Paton came into sight, running up the drive, but before he reached the gates, Jinny and Shantih had trotted out of sight down the road.

"They were wolves," Jinny told her mother. "I went back to check."

"Wolves? Are you really sure?"

"I am positive. They're so worried in case anyone finds out about them that now I've seen them I've not to go back. I was only standing looking at them, and they weren't a bit bothered, just lying there snoozing when this gamekeeper bloke comes up with a gun."

"Jinny," warned Mrs. Manders.

"With a gun," repeated Jinny. "Blows his top because I was standing there, tells Lady Gilbert and now I've never to go back."

"It all sounds most peculiar to me," said Mrs. Manders, returning to the letter she had been writing before Jinny had burst in upon her.

"It is," said Jinny, "but I don't care. I'm glad I don't have to go back. Gives me more time to school Shantih for Miss Tuke's cross-country."

Mrs. Manders' ears had picked out one word. "Why don't you do some of your homework now?" she suggested. "You always seem to have so much at the weekends. Do some of it now and you'll all have less to do tomorrow."

Jinny groaned, a vast, camel-weary groan.

"Dad and Mike won't be back until sevenish. We'll eat then. That will give you almost two hours."

With her school bag slung over her back, a cheese sandwich in one hand and a mug of hot chocolate in the other, Jinny plodded upstairs to her room. Kelly appeared and followed her up.

All Jinny's school books were piled on the table in her room. She had acquired the table so that she would be able to do her homework without being disturbed. It was at the far end of the room, next to the mural of the Red Horse, under the window that looked out over the moors.

Jinny sat down on the sill of her window that looked out over the sea, as far away from her school books as she could manage. She shared her sandwich with Kelly and drank her chocolate while she looked down at the field where Shantih and Bramble were grazing side by side. The sound of Petra's piano playing drifted up from below.

Jinny thought about Lady Gilbert and the wolves, and wondered what Ken would have made of it.

"I'll draw them and send it to him," Jinny told Kelly. "That wouldn't be a letter. He said drawings would be O.K."

Jinny pictured the wolves in her mind's eye, their thick coats, yellow eyes, intelligent faces and the wildness of them. They were completely different to any dog that Jinny had ever seen, no matter how savage. She remembered the first time she had seen them, how they had hurled themselves against the wire netting, slavering and leaping into the air.

"That's strange," Jinny said aloud, stopping herself in mid-thought. She went carefully back in her mind, seeing the wolves of the first afternoon and as they had been today. "I'm certain," she said.

Last Saturday afternoon there had been six wolves, today there had only been five.

CHAPTER FIVE

On Sunday Jinny spent the morning in her bedroom, staring in horrified mystification at her Algebra textbook. She had only been learning Algebra since she had gone to Inverburgh school and already she was totally lost. There was no chance of Jinny ever understanding Algebra. The years of Algebra which lay ahead of her were a grim prospect.

In the last hour before lunch Jinny had read a chapter

49

of history, drawn a map of Britain showing rainfall and another showing temperature and began to learn a poem for English.

"I'll finish that on the bus," she declared, putting all her books back into her school bag.

She made a quick check through the window on Shantih and then went down to lunch.

"Is someone going to take Kelly for a walk this afternoon?" Mrs. Manders asked. "He's spent all morning lying outside Ken's room."

"I'll take him with me," Jinny said. "I'm going to do some jumping. He can stay in the field with me and then I'll go for a ride up the moor and give him a good run."

"The same as he had the last time you took him?" asked Petra sweetly.

"I thought Mr. MacKenzie had stopped you from jumping in his field. Didn't he say that you were ploughing it up too much now that the ground's so wet?" asked Mr. Manders.

Jinny hadn't wanted to remember this. "Shouldn't think he'll mind. Not seeing it's for Miss Tuke's competition. He likes Miss Tuke."

"Better ask first," said Jinny's mother. "No one has been for the milk today, you could get it and ask him at the same time."

"I've been swotting away all morning," complained Jinny, "and now I have to go for the milk. That's not a bit fair."

"I've been chopping wood," said Mike, "and that's more like work than sitting up in your bedroom reading."

"I was not reading. I was working. Wait till you get to Inverburgh."

"How do we know?" insisted Mike. "Now that we can't see you working I don't think you do anything. You just lie on your bed and read or draw."

"Believe what you like," said Jinny. "It won't alter the facts. I have been working all morning." She finished her last mouthful of apple crumble. "Can I go now?" she asked her mother. "I'll take Kelly."

"All right," said Mrs. Manders. "The milk can is in the pantry."

50

Jinny collected Kelly and the milk can and set out for the farm.

"It's no use," she told Kelly, "going on being miserable. My mother is getting fed up with your moping. Where will you be if she tips you out? All alone in the gales and snows, that's where."

Kelly trotted despondently at Jinny's side. He did not appear to be listening.

"You are better with us than alone in this cruel world. I am telling you, you had better make the most of us because we're all you've got. Ken has gone."

At the sound of Ken's name, Kelly's head lifted, he looked round wildly, moist nose twitching, tail swinging in anticipation.

"No, Kelly, no," cried Jinny. "I did not say that. No, he's not here." She crouched down to comfort Kelly. For a moment the dog laid his head on Jinny's shoulder and she felt his lost, desolate misery.

"If I could, I'd bring him back, but I can't and nor can you," Jinny told him. "We haven't heard from him either, so you're no worse than we are." She hugged Kelly to her, trying to comfort him.

They passed the field where Sue and Jinny had built their show jumping course in the summer. Their jumps were stacked in a corner of the field. Only Jinny and Sue would have known they were jumps, anyone else would have thought they were a pile of junk.

"I'll need to build two or three jumps in the driest bit," Jinny thought, looking at the state of the field. One end had almost gone back to swamp and even the other end was patched with mud and pools of water.

When they reached the farmyard, Mr. MacKenzie was standing in the byre doorway, smoking his pipe and staring out at the sky.

"Hullo," said Jinny.

"Aye," said the farmer, taking Jinny's milk can and going to fill it.

"Thanks," said Jinny when he brought it back to her, and she turned to stand beside him in the doorway.

The farmer did not speak which Jinny knew was a bad sign. He was wanting her to go away.

"Have you heard that Miss Tuke is starting a Trekking Club?" Jinny asked cautiously.

"Aye. No fool like an old fool. She'd be better finding herself a man than carrying on with all that nonsense."

"Now you know you like her. She makes you laugh."

"She'll be the queer old bird that one if she doesn't look out."

"Well, anyway," said Jinny, "no matter what you think about her she has started a Trekking Club and next Sunday we're having a sort of jumping competition and what I want to ask you is – can I put up three or four jumps in your field to practise over this afternoon?"

"No," said Mr. MacKenzie.

"I'll take them down when I've finished."

"And my good ground will be like the bog itself by that time. No, I'll not be having it."

Jinny knew better than to argue.

"Do you know Lady Gilbert?" she asked, changing the subject.

"Are you telling me you've been hob-nobbing with that one?"

Jinny nodded.

"It's the odd company you choose. One as mad as the other. It's your mother should be putting the hems on you, she should."

"I'm not to go back," said Jinny. "She chased me."

Jinny wondered if she should tell Mr. MacKenzie about the wolves but decided it would take too long, and probably he wouldn't believe her.

"Couldn't I just put up three jumps at the dry end of the field? You know it's the only field that's flat enough for jumping and I promise that whenever the ground gets too churned up I'll stop."

"Three jumps?"

"Well, maybe four and two bits of wall."

Mr. MacKenzie didn't answer. He continued to stare into space while Kelly stirred impatiently at the end of his binder twine.

"While I have you here I'll be telling you something about that dog. Don't you be letting him on the hill now. Keep him ben the house for there's been sheep worried over Garthlarnock side and if the farmers there were to be seeing a stray dog on their hill they'd have the bullet in him the second they clapped eyes on him."

"Kelly wouldn't chase sheep," stated Jinny. "He's not like that. I told you."

"Well, I'll tell you this. Jock Hendry was by yesterday and he was asking if I knew of any grey dogs near here. He'd seen one on the hill near his place and the description he was giving me fitted yon Kelly like his skin."

"It couldn't have been Kelly. He never leaves the house just now," said Jinny, hoping that she sounded more confident than she felt. "Besides, the Hendry's farm is miles from here."

"Och, not to a dog the size of Kelly. He could be there and back in a morning and your mother never noticing he'd gone. It's the cunning they get when they're at the sheep killing."

"Kelly wouldn't kill sheep. He's used to being on the moors with Ken where there's sheep all round him."

"Aye, when Ken was here, but now what's he at? Glooming around with nothing to fill his time. It's the touch of occupation he'd be welcoming, that same dog."

"And I'm telling you he'd never go near a sheep," said Jinny furiously. Picking up her milk can and jerking Kelly to his feet she turned and left Mr. MacKenzie.

"Half an hour round those jumps," Mr. MacKenzie called after her. "Not a moment more. I'll have the glasses on you."

"I'm after hearing you," Jinny shouted back without looking round.

Jinny put the milk can down by the field gate, climbed over it herself and was just about to organize Kelly through the wire at the side of the gate when Kelly gave one effortless bound over it.

"You don't realise how big he is," Jinny thought. "We're so used to having him in the house we forget, but he is big – nearly as big as an Alsatian, nearly as big as one of the Gilbert's wolves."

Jinny considered letting Kelly off his binder twine but decided that if she did and he ran away that would be the end of her afternoon's jumping.

"When I've finished jumping we'll go for a run round the hill," Jinny promised Kelly as she tied him to the gatepost. "You stay there just now."

Kelly grumbled to himself but settled down.

"Now," thought Jinny and splodged across the field to where the jumps were stacked. She dragged one pole out from the pile and took it to the far end of the field where she fixed it along the top of a wall.

"That's as good as a water jump," she thought, looking with satisfaction at the flood water on both sides of the obstacle.

Then she fetched the hen coops and put them in front of another wall to make a spread jump.

"I'll go straight down the field, over the water jump, up the side of the other field, over this spread and then I'll make three jumps at the top of the field," Jinny decided.

When she had finished building the three jumps they looked quite cross-countryish. She had built one – deck-chairs and poles – on top of an outcrop of rock so that it had a drop landing, and one next to a hawthorn bush so it was woody-looking. She marked a water jump over a pool of water and immediately after it a pile of cans, poles and rotting straw bales.

"Shantih will hardly see those," Jinny told Kelly. "But I don't suppose Miss Tuke's will be any higher. Anyway, it's not the height that's our problem, it's staying in control between the jumps."

"Have you got the milk?" Mike asked, coming into the stable as Jinny groomed Shantih.

"Blow it," said Jinny. "I've left it by the flipping field gate."

"There's none left," said Mike. "I'll come with you and fetch it."

"Oh, thanks," said Jinny gratefully. "You could lead Kelly."

"O.K.," said Mike. "Can you cope with Kelly when you're riding Shantih?"

"No trouble," said Jinny.

"He'd be all right off his lead," said Mike, crouching down to untie the binder twine.

"No," said Jinny, bringing Shantih out into the yard.

54

"Mr. MacKenzie was going on about dogs chasing the sheep. He says they've seen a grey dog on the moors so you'd better hang on to him."

"Chase sheep?" said Mike. "Kelly wouldn't chase sheep. Must have been some other dog." But he kept Kelly on the lead.

In the field, Jinny trotted Shantih in circles and figures of eight. Mike leaned on the gate, watching. Shantih was behaving well, paying attention to Jinny, concentrating on her rider.

"Remember what she was like in the spring?" Mike shouted. "Nothing but rearing and bucking all the time. You spent all your time falling off."

"She has improved," Jinny agreed, touching Shantih into a collected canter. "And she's pretty fit being ridden to Glenbost every day."

After Jinny had cantered about the field for ten minutes she decided it was time to start jumping.

"Or Mr. MacKenzie will be waving from the farm shouting. 'Come in number one'," she told Mike. "You be the starter. I'm ready now."

"Three, two, one. Go!" yelled Mike, making Kelly jump to his feet barking.

Shantih leapt forward as Jinny shortened her reins, sank her weight down into her stirrups and urged her on. They went down the field at a pounding gallop, splashing fountains from the soaking ground.

Jinny sat tight, riding Shantih at the first jump – the wall with the pole on top. Jinny expected Shantih to canter in close to the wall and hop over it, to land in the water on the other side. Shantih goggled and leapt, stretching herself in a flowing arc as she took off before the flood water in the field and landed far out into the other field, again clearing the water.

Turning Shantih up the field, Jinny was laughing with delight. It was a week or two since she had jumped Shantih. School, Ken's departure and Miss Tuke's Trekking Club had all got in the way. Now there was nothing else in Jinny's head but the force of her galloping horse and the thrust and power of her jumping.

They tore up the edge of the other field. "Steady,

steady," Jinny whispered, turning her horse at the wall but Shantih had already seen the hen coops on the other side of the wall and knew it was a jump. Snatching the reins from Jinny's grasp she flew over it with feet to spare.

Just in time, Jinny managed to gather in her reins and turn Shantih at the drop jump. The tattered canvas from the deckchairs flapped in the wind. Shantih stopped suddenly, sniffed suspiciously at the flagging canvas, realised that it was nothing to be afraid of and launched herself into the air. Jinny felt as if she were dropping down a bottomless lift shaft. It seemed minutes before Shantih landed and even longer before Jinny's stomach was back in its proper place.

Shantih paid no attention at all to the hawthorn-bush, popping over it as if she could hardly be bothered to jump such a silly little thing. She treated the jump across the water and the last pile of poles and bales as a double; stretching herself over the water then putting in one stride and soaring clear over the jump.

"Didn't she do well?" demanded Mike. "She really can jump. It's no effort to her. Don't think you make much difference to her. She'd jump just the same if you weren't there."

"She would not," said Jinny breathlessly. "You try riding her and you'd soon know how much I do. She felt as if she jumped miles into the air at that second wall."

"She did. Easily three times as high as the wall. Are you going round again?"

"No," decided Jinny. "That will do her for today. No point in mashing up Mr. MacKenzie's good mud when I don't need to. I'll go for a ride on the moors and take Kelly with me."

"Gosh the milk," said Mike, remembering suddenly. "I forgot about it. Better dash." Handing Kelly to Jinny, he ran off down the lane.

"I've finished. Thanks," Jinny called to Mr. MacKenzie as she rode through his yard. "I only rode round once. And I've got Kelly on his lead."

"It'll be the bargain lead that one," said Mr. MacKenzie who was still staring out from his byre door, it being the Sabbath and not a day for work.

"Free lead," said Jinny.

"Be minding what I told you now. Keep that dog away from the sheep or there's the bullet waiting with his name on it."

"I will," said Jinny, thinking that Mr. MacKenzie was making a fuss about nothing for she was certain that Kelly would never chase sheep.

When she was a little way up the hill, Jinny dismounted and untied Kelly.

"Now you've got to stay with me," she told him. "Stay in close."

Jinny remounted and rode Shantih up the hill at a steady walk. She kept looking round to check that Kelly was still with her. Sheep sprang up in sudden, bundling panics but Kelly hardly glanced at them. Even when Jinny trotted, Kelly stayed close beside her.

Jinny stopped at the top of a rise in the moorland. She dismounted and told Kelly to go for a run by himself. Yapping and leaping, Kelly bounded through the crisp, golden-red bracken; throwing himself down flat into it so that he vanished from Jinny's sight, then suddenly leaping, twisting into the air for sheer delight.

Jinny was just about to call him in and set off back to Finmory when she heard men's voices and the tramp of feet. It was so unusual for there to be any strangers on the moors that Jinny froze with instant fear. In a whisper she called Kelly to her and took a tighter hold on Shantih's reins.

Three men came into sight, circling a rocky hump in the moorland, a little way from her. Two were young men that Jinny didn't know. The third man Jinny recognised at once. He was Mr. Paton, the wolf keeper from Bendarroch.

Jinny tightened her grip on Kelly's collar. She could not imagine what they were doing here. A ray of winter sunlight sparkled on the barrels of Mr. Paton's gun and Jinny shuddered, the hair on the nape of her neck rising and cold shivers running down her spine as she watched them tramp out of sight, climbing higher into the hills.

CHAPTER SIX

Jinny rode into Miss Tuke's yard the next Sunday morning with Kelly trotting beside her at the end of his binder twine.

"Good show!" Miss Tuke greeted her. "Stayed on top this time."

Jinny managed a sickly smile.

"Not too bright an idea bringing a dog with you," Miss Tuke added. "Did you lead him all the way?"

Jinny opened her mouth to say, "No, he flew," but thought the better of it and only said that she had had to bring Kelly because her mother was worried about him moping and thought a change would do him good.

"Can't take him on to the course," stated Miss Tuke, with an eye on one of the ladies who was hopping along with her foot in the stirrup while her grey Highland walked across the yard. "I'll have my hands full coping with the nags, never mind stray dogs."

"He won't be stray," said Jinny.

"He won't be there," said Miss Tuke. "I'll find you somewhere to leave him. Be best."

"But . . ."

"No more to be said," Miss Tuke turned away to urge the lady upwards with shouts of "Spring, spring from your toe."

Jinny looked round the yard. It seemed to be full of riders and ponies and Jinny realised that there were going to be quite a few spectators. All the riders seemed to have brought parents or friends with them.

"She could have let me have Kelly," Jinny thought. "I don't even have anyone who knows me."

"Good morning," said a man's voice behind her.

Kelly growled, deep in his throat, and Jinny twisted round in her saddle to see who had spoken.

Hard, bleak eyes stared up at her. It was Ralph Gilbert.

Jinny muttered a reply, closed her heels against Shantih's sides and trotted away from him.

"What right has he to be here?" Jinny thought furiously. "Miss Tuke's Trekking Club has got nothing to do with him."

She felt a clutch of nerves in her stomach and didn't really know whether it was the sudden appearance of Ralph Gilbert or the thought of the cross-country.

It really was going to be a competition. Even if the cross-country jumps weren't very high she would still have to jump them in front of Miss Tuke. Jinny knew that Miss Tuke thought Shantih was flighty and out of control for most of the time. If she ran away with Jinny today it would only confirm Miss Tuke's opinion and Jinny did not want that to happen. She knew that Miss Tuke would be bound to mention it the next time she met her parents.

"Be sensible," Jinny said to her horse. "Be good. It's only the littlest comp., in fact it's not really a competition at all."

But Shantih wasn't listening. Her neck was arched as she gazed around with wild eyes, pawing at the ground with her forelegs.

"She is fresh," said Miss Tuke, regarding Shantih with a wary eye. "Too many oats by the looks of things."

"She's fit," said Jinny. "She has to be fit to take me to Glenbost every day. And I have to feed her. I can't starve her."

"No one is suggesting starvation," said Miss Tuke. "Ask someone to hold her for you until we find a home for that dog."

Jinny dismounted reluctantly.

"Please couldn't Kelly stay with us?" she said.

Kelly gazed up at Miss Tuke. Through his shaggy hair his eyes were fixed on Miss Tuke's face. His nose quivered, even his front paws, placed neatly together, seemed to be pleading to be allowed to stay with Jinny. He wuffed at Miss Tuke, telling her how well he would behave if she would only change her mind and not shut him up.

"Don't argue," said Miss Tuke sharply. "A dog running loose among ponies – absolutely lethal – especially when you're dealing with novices."

"But Kelly won't be loose . . ."

"Bring him over here," commanded Miss Tuke.

Jinny gave Shanthi's reins to one of the parents who looked competent and, taking Kelly with her, set out after Miss Tuke.

Kelly dragged his feet and pulled against the twine lead.

"I'm sorry," Jinny told him. "Honestly I am. I thought you could sit and watch and enjoy it all. It isn't my fault."

Hearing Jinny's voice soften, Kelly pushed his head against her hand, his tail wagging furiously, telling her that he would never dream of causing any trouble.

"How is that Ken boy getting on?" Miss Tuke asked as Jinny caught up with her. "Rather an odd lad if you ask me."

Jinny didn't want to have to tell Miss Tuke that they still hadn't heard from Ken.

"Fine," she muttered. "Are the jumps going to be very high in the cross-country?"

"High enough," said Miss Tuke. "That's what you wanted, wasn't it? Should think you three girls will be about the same standard. The oldest boy is joining you. Hasn't jumped much before but he wants to have a shot. Now, here's the place for your dog. Be quite safe in here." Miss Tuke opened the door of a rather broken-down shed. "Fetch some water and leave him here."

Jinny looked round the shed without enthusiasm. She had wanted Kelly to have a happy day but now it looked as if he would have been better at home.

"Please couldn't I tie him up where he could watch us jumping?"

"Certainly not. I've told you, dangerous thing a loose dog running about where there's horses. Fetch the water quickly and let's get a move on."

Jinny brought a full bucket of water and set it down inside the shed. She told Kelly that he would have to stay there. Kelly regarded her with sad eyes, his ears drooping and his tail tucked between his legs.

"I am sorry," Jinny told him, crouching down to stroke him and untie his binder twine. "It won't be for too long.

Honestly. I'll be back whenever I can but you must stay here."

Kelly whimpered, rubbing his head against her hand, licking her fingers, still hoping that Jinny would change her mind.

"Stay," said Jinny, forcing herself to sound severe. "Stay there."

Kelly groaned to himself and lay down, but his eyes watched Jinny and Miss Tuke leaving him, hoping every second that they would call his name; still certain, until they closed the door on him, that they couldn't really mean to shut him up and leave him alone.

Jinny took Shantih back from the parent, who looked very relieved to be handing her over.

"You're welcome to that one," he told Jinny. "Done everything except stand on its head."

"Thank you for holding her," Jinny said politely, hoping that Miss Tuke wasn't listening. "I think she knows it is a competition, that's why she's so excited."

Jinny mounted quickly, hoping that having her rider in the saddle would settle Shantih, but it didn't. When Miss Tuke clapped her hands and banged her fist against a feed bin to get everyone's attention, Shantih reared up, her forelegs striking the air above a sea of upturned, shocked faces.

"She's only showing off," Jinny said loudly, hoping they would all hear. "It's because she's an Arab that she gets so excited."

Miss Tuke snorted contemptuously and got on with her announcement.

"Handy Pony Trekker is to be in the bottom paddock. It will be judged on style and control and I am the final-decision judge. Handy Pony Trekker will be first and our Cross-Country Course second. I'll be press-ganging some of our spectators to act as jump stewards. So be prepared."

"Only too pleased to help," said one of the parents.

"Fine," enthused Miss Tuke. "Handy Pony Trekkers lead on to the bottom paddock and cross-country riders gather round."

Moira on Snuff, Sara on Pym – a dapple-grey pony,

61

Peter Hay on one of Miss Tuke's trekkers and Jinny on Shantih, gathered round.

"There's a flat bit of ground over there," Miss Tuke said, pointing through a gate. "I suggest that you take advantage of being second and give your nags a bit of a school. You'll want to have them well under control for my cross-country. Shouldn't take too long to put the trekkers through their paces and then we'll walk the course."

"I want to watch my brothers," said Peter.

"Please yourself," said Miss Tuke. "With your vast experience . . ."

She left them to judge the trekkers. Peter shrugged his shoulders and followed her, while Sara, Moira and Jinny rode into the field.

"Have you seen the course?" asked Sara.

Jinny and Moira shook their heads.

"Well I'll bet you it's enormous. I've had three jumping lessons from Tukey and you should have seen the things she had us jumping. You can see a bit of the course up there." Sarah pointed to where they could just make out several timber jumps on the hillside.

The jumps looked very big and very solid. Bigger than anything Shantih was used to jumping. Jinny felt her stomach curl with excitement. It was going to be a real cross-country course.

She rode Shantih away from the others and began to school her. At first Jinny kept the mare at a slow trot, sitting down in her saddle and pushing her horse into her bit. Jinny rode her in circles and figure-eights until she felt Shantih relax, felt the rhythm of her trot flowing smoothly through her horse.

"We're going over to see how the others are getting on," Moira shouted. "Are you coming?"

Jinny had been concentrating so hard on her horse that she had totally forgotten about everything except Shantih's stride and balance. She jerked back to reality at the sound of Moira's voice.

"No," Jinny shouted back. "I want to canter for a bit."

"O.K." replied Moira, trotting after Sara who was riding through the gate.

Shantih whinnied and bucked to follow the other horses

but Jinny ignored her protests and rode her round in their schooling circle, letting her canter on until she was calm again and paying attention to her rider.

Jinny went on cantering for about another ten minutes. She was just beginning to think that Shantih had done enough when she saw Ralph Gilbert walking through the gate.

"What on earth does he want," Jinny thought irritably. She brought Shantih to a halt and watched as he walked straight towards them.

For a second she considered galloping away to escape from him but told herself not to be so stupid. There was nothing Ralph Gilbert could do to harm her, not here in Miss Tuke's field with everyone in earshot. Nevertheless, Jinny knew that she was afraid. There was something heartless and cold about Ralph Gilbert; something that Jinny couldn't quite put her finger on but made her blood run chill when she saw him.

He came striding up to Shantih, his blank eyes fixed on Jinny's face. As he reached them his claw hand pounced on Shantih's rein and held her tightly at the ring of her bit.

"Let go of my horse," Jinny cried indignantly, but Ralph Gilbert ignored her.

"I want a word with you," he said. "I think we have one or two things to say to each other."

"What about?"

"I think you know."

"If it's about my paintings I don't care whether you want me to paint your Arabs or not."

"You know perfectly well that it's not about your paintings. It's about your little visit to my private kennels. You saw my dogs, didn't you, you nasty, spying, little nuisance?"

Suddenly Ralph Gilbert's other hand shot out and grabbed Jinny by the shoulder of her jacket. He forced her towards him until her face was within inches of his own.

"Should I hear any gossip about my dogs I shall know who started it. My animals are my own affair. Do I make myself quite clear."

"Let me go!" yelled Jinny, struggling to free herself.

"Keep your mouth shut," Ralph Gilbert threatened. "Or . . ."

"Jinny, Jinny," called Moira's voice. "We're starting. Come on."

Instantly Ralph Gilbert released his hold on Jinny and Shantih, and as Moira rode through the gate he was hurrying away.

"That was Lady Gilbert's son, wasn't it?" asked Moira curiously, as Jinny joined her. "What did he want?"

"Oh, nothing," said Jinny. "He's a bit crazy if you ask me."

She urged Shantih on down to the paddock. "He was trying to scare me off," Jinny thought as she rode. "Some dogs! They were wolves. That's why he was so mad that I'd seen them. Keeping them shut away like that and not wanting people to know what he's doing." Jinny shivered at the thought of the forbidding wall hiding away the wolves; at the thought of Ralph Gilbert thinking he could do what he liked just because he lived at Bendarroch.

"Over here," called Miss Tuke and Jinny thrust all thoughts of Bendarroch out of her mind. She was going to ride a cross-country course for the first time in her life and she wasn't going to allow Ralph Gilbert to spoil Shantih's chances.

"I built this course especially for you," Miss Tuke was telling them. "An experiment. If you do well round it I'm thinking of expanding my next year's trekking to include cross-country riding. Nothing too difficult. The sort of thing that most trekkers could tackle. Now, you start here."

They all followed Miss Tuke up a narrow track to the first jump. It was a fairly low jump of parallel poles but immediately after it the track turned sharply right to a jump of gorse bushes and oil drums.

"And it's a drop," said Jinny, imagining herself charging up to it completely out of control.

After the drop they went across the hillside over two jumps built into the stone walls. The first was a stile and the second was poles with a ditch on the landing side. After the walls there was a sheep pen making an in and out, followed by an enormous spread.

"How about it?" Miss Tuke laughed, seeing the expressions on their faces. "From here on you follow the flags down the hillside and back round to the paddock. There's two more walls to jump but if you get round this lot you'll never notice the walls."

Walking back to Shantih, Jinny felt a cold sinking in her stomach. It really was a cross-country course. Far harder than anything Shantih had ever tried before. She had jumped one of Mr. MacKenzie's farm gates, which had been higher than any of Miss Tuke's jumps, but that had been a single jump, not a series of jumps on rough going like this course. The others all looked as if they were thinking the same thing.

"I warned you," said Sara. "Miss Tuke doesn't believe in tiny jumps. When she builds courses you can see them."

"You're allowed three refusals at each jump but that's all or the take-offs will be churned into soup. Any questions?" Miss Tuke said as they gathered at the start.

"Are you timing us?" asked Moira.

"No," said Miss Tuke. "So take it steady, especially at the drop and the sheep pen."

"Some hopes," said Moira. "You know what he's like."

"Sara, you go first, then Peter, Moira and Jinny last. I'll count you down from five, blow my whistle and you're off."

Sara rode with long stirrups and a deep seat, keeping her Highland at a steady canter. As they came to the first jump Pym slowed to a trot, stuck out his head suspiciously and stopped. Sara rode at it again, Pym catapulted over and stopped dead on the far side, depositing Sara into the mud.

"Little twister," said Miss Tuke. "He can jump perfectly when he wants to."

They saw Sara remount and then she was out of sight, hidden by the turn in the track, but in seconds she reappeared, so that they knew she must have cleared the drop without a refusal.

"That's him started. He'll clear the rest without a murmur," said Miss Tuke.

She was right. When Sara finished the course she had only had one more refusal at the sheep pen.

C

Snuff and Moira were next. Already Snuff was sweating and dancing as he waited at the start.

"She'd better look out at the drop," Sara said to Jinny. "I wasn't going all that fast and it felt like a lift shaft."

"Expect we'll go into orbit," said Jinny, knowing how fast Shantih jumped.

Snuff charged up to the jumps then either refused or rushed past. They had two refusals at every jump and three at the sheep pen, which meant elimination.

"Bad luck," said Jinny as Moira rejoined them. "But don't worry. I'll do exactly the same thing. You wait and see."

Peter was riding a heavy-dark brown Highland with soup plate feet who cantered steadily over the obstacles and although Peter was left behind at every jump he only had two refusals.

"Are you ready, Jinny?" called Miss Tuke.

"Yes," said Jinny as she brought Shantih to the start, feeling anything but ready. Her hard hat was suddenly too tight and her stirrups felt uneven but it was too late to change them now. Too late to do anything but ride.

"It's all happened too soon," thought Jinny desperately. "Shantih's not ready for this. I never thought it would be anything like this . . ."

Miss Tuke's whistle cut through Jinny's last-minute panic and instinctively she sat down in the saddle and urged Shantih forward.

The Arab's long-reaching stride swallowed up the ground and almost before Jinny realised that they had actually started, the first jump loomed before them. They were going too fast but Jinny knew that to check Shantih would be fatal.

"On you go," she whispered and felt her horse reach forward, clearing the low jump with a leap so smooth that Jinny hardly knew she had left the ground.

With the first jump behind her Jinny was enjoying herself. Delight in Shantih's speed sang through her as they swung round the bend, and in two strides Shantih was soaring over the gorse jump. If there was a drop Jinny didn't feel it, Shantih had cleared it with such a flying leap.

66

They galloped out over the grass to the stile in the wall, reached it and it fell away behind them. Jinny had seen Badminton riders galloping like this, their horses so full of going that the ground seemed to flow beneath them.

Seeing the ditch on the far side of the second wall, Shantih stretched out to clear it and landed far beyond. Jinny had lost all sense of time. Jumps and stewards flashed past unseen as they flew round.

Shantih timed the sheep pen exactly, clearing it as if it had been no more than cavalletti. She gathered herself for the spread and soared over it with feet to spare. In seconds they were at the finish, Shantih taking the two walls in the course as if they hadn't existed.

They were round clear. Riding back to the others, Jinny could hardly believe it, hardly heard the applause or Miss Tuke's praise for the voice in her own head telling her that Shantih had made it. No longer could anyone say that she was wild or uncontrollable. She was a cross-country horse now. The partnership that Jinny had always dreamt about was beginning to come true. Sliding to the ground, Jinny threw her arms round Shantih's neck and buried her face in her mane. She had no words.

"Back to the yard for the presentation of rosettes," Miss Tuke told them and everyone began to walk back to the stables.

"You were going like the clappers. You'd have known all about it if she'd come down with you," Miss Tuke said as she walked beside Jinny, but the way she looked at Shantih had changed.

"She never felt like slipping," said Jinny. "I suppose she's so used to galloping on the moor that she never notices the rough going."

"Might be something to do with your riding as well," laughed Miss Tuke.

When they were all gathered in the yard, Miss Tuke asked Mrs. Hay to present the rosettes.

"And now the Cross Country," Mrs. Hay said when she had presented the rosettes for the Handy Trekking Pony. "First, Miss Jennifer Manders on Shantih."

Jinny led Shantih forward to receive her rosette. She

said thank you and smiled, feeling floating and unreal, then turned back to the sound of clapping.

As Jinny looked round the little group of people she realised that Ralph Gilbert had gone. "Bet he only came to warn me about the wolves," she thought. "Trying to tell me they were dogs." And instantly Jinny thought "Kelly". A swell of guilt flooded over her. She had completely forgotten about him.

Peter was second and Sara third. When they had been presented with their rosettes, Miss Tuke thanked everyone for coming, reminded the Club members that there would be a winter trek a week on Saturday and said that sandwiches and hot soup would be served in her study.

"I'll be back in a minute," Jinny told Shantih as she took her into an empty box and loosened her girths. "I've got to go and get Kelly. He's not staying in that shed for a minute longer."

Jinny shut the loose box door and ran full tilt round to the shed where she had left Kelly.

"Kelly," she called. "Come on, boy. There's a good dog."

As she reached the shed there was no sound of Kelly, no barking or scratching at the door. Only silence. As she pushed the door open Jinny thought he must still be in a corner, sulking.

"Kelly, come on, Kelly."

Jinny strained her eyes peering into the dark of the shed.

"Kelly," she called again desperately. "Kelly!"

But Kelly wasn't there. The shed was empty.

CHAPTER SEVEN

"Kelly's gone. He's not in the shed. He's got out," Jinny shouted as she burst into Miss Tuke's study.

They all looked round at her in surprise, mugs of soup and sandwiches suspended in their hands.

"He's gone. He's got out."

"He can't have," said Miss Tuke.

"He has," cried Jinny. "He has."

"Are you sure?" demanded Miss Tuke irritably. "If you shut the door securely there's no way he could have got out."

"Honestly he's not there. Come and see."

Annoyed by Jinny's disturbance, Miss Tuke hurried on ahead of her to the shed. For a second as Miss Tuke pushed the door open Jinny thought that it was just possible that she might have been wrong, that Kelly would be there, but of course he wasn't. The shed was empty.

"Well, he's not there," said Miss Tuke, stating the obvious. "Are you sure you shut the door properly?"

"Utterly positive."

"It was rather a stupid thing to do bringing him here in the first place."

"I only wanted him to enjoy himself for a change," muttered Jinny, thinking that if Miss Tuke had allowed her to tie Kelly up to the paddock fence this would never have happened.

"Ah," exclaimed Miss Tuke. "Here's how he managed it."

One of the shed windows was broken and a piece of sacking had been nailed across it. A corner of the sacking had been torn and chewed. Grey dog hairs on one of the nails confirmed that this was how Kelly had made his escape.

"Varmint," said Miss Tuke. "He's probably back at Finmory by now."

"He could be anywhere," said Jinny. "He's looking for Ken. All he wants is to be back with Ken." Suddenly Jinny realised that she shouldn't be standing there chatting as if time didn't matter. "I've got to get home and try to find him. He mustn't get on to the moor with the sheep."

"Does he chase them?"

"No, of course he doesn't. It's the farmers. They'd shoot any dog they saw on the moors even if it wasn't near their sheep."

"Can't blame them," said Miss Tuke. "Sheep are their living. Pretty valuable thing today, a sheep."

Jinny couldn't wait to argue.

69

"I've got to go," she said, and, pushing past Miss Tuke, she ran round to the stables.

"We've got to find Kelly," she told Shantih as she tightened her girths and led her out of the box. "I should never have left him in that shed."

"Where are you off to?" called Moira, who had come out to make sure that Snuff wasn't breaking down Miss Tuke's box door.

"Got to get home," Jinny shouted back as she rode out of the yard.

Nothing mattered now except to get home and find out if Kelly was there. There was always a chance that he might have gone home or that someone might have recognised him and taken him back to Finmory. But these were only faint hopes. It was only too likely that Kelly would be on the hills searching for Ken.

Jinny urged Shantih into a faster trot. Her watch said half-past two which was unlikely to be the correct time, but since it was still ticking Jinny thought it would be more or less right. She would be home before it was dark and would be able to search for Kelly while there was still daylight left.

Suddenly Shantih stumbled. For a horrible second, as she was pitched forward, Jinny was sure that Shantih was coming down on her knees, but somehow she managed to stay on her feet. She lurched forward and came to a trembling halt. Jinny slid quickly to the ground.

"Shantih," she whispered, rubbing her horse's soft muzzle. "Poor girl. What happened? Did you trip?"

Jinny could see nothing in the road that could have made Shantih stumble. A van came towards them and Jinny pulled Shantih into the side. The Arab came reluctantly. She was dead lame in her off foreleg.

Jinny picked up her foot and scraped with her fingers at the mud and dirt compressed into the sole of Shantih's hoof but her fingers were not strong enough to loosen the hard-packed mass.

"Blast and botheration," Jinny muttered furiously. "If I were a properly organised person I'd have a hoofpick. Shantih, stand still," she cried as the Arab dragged her foot from Jinny's grasp and swung her quarters into the middle of the narrow road. "Do that in front of a car and you'll only be half a horse. Now stand. Stand still."

Looping her arm through the reins, Jinny searched along the bottom of the hedgerow for some sort of stone that would do instead of a hoofpick. She found a long shard of flint, tested it on the ground to make sure that it was strong enough and decided that it would do.

"Now hold still," she said severely to Shantih as she picked up her off forefoot, and, holding it by the tip of the hoof, began to pick it out. Mud and dirt scattered to the ground and Jinny saw what was the matter.

"Oh no," she cried. "Why did that have to happen now, just when I've got to get home?"

Jammed between the frog of Shantih's foot and her shoe was a large, sharp-edged stone. Jinny poked at it furiously but it was wedged solidly into place. She tried to force the end of her stone hoofpick underneath it but it wouldn't budge. There was no way that Jinny could move it without a proper hoofpick. Clenching her teeth with irritation, Jinny let go of Shantih's foot.

"Back to Miss Tuke's," she told Shantih and began to lead her horse back to the trekking centre.

"And there'll be such a fuss," Jinny thought as they made their infuriatingly slow progress along the road.

When Jinny reached the yard Moira was the first to see her.

"What's wrong?" she shouted.

"She's lame. Got a stone in her hoof. Could you tell Miss Tuke?"

"Nasty," said Miss Tuke when she saw the stone. "Hold on a sec till I find a hoofpick."

It only took Miss Tuke a minute to get the stone out.

"Try her now."

Jinny led Shantih forward. She was still lame.

"Pity you didn't notice it before you trotted her on the road," said Miss Tuke. "No foot no horse. True saying that. Need to lead her home and rest her till she's sound, or leave her here until next weekend."

"Oh no, I'd better take her back to Finmory," said Jinny hurriedly. She couldn't bear the thought of Shantih being away from her unless it was absolutely necessary.

"Off with you then," said Miss Tuke, "or it'll be dark before you're back. And carry a hoofpick with you from now on."

"Will do," promised Jinny. "Thank you for getting the stone out."

Even on the soft forestry roads Shantih was still lame. She dragged behind Jinny, refusing to walk out, until Jinny's arms ached with pulling her along.

"Not far now," Jinny told her, which wasn't true. They couldn't have been more than half way home and already the October evening was blackening the pines into stark sillhouettes against a louring grey sky.

"Don't think it," Jinny warned herself, but already it was too late. She had thought it; thought that it was a night for wolves and she shivered suddenly.

Now that the light was fading, Shantih began to prop and shy at pine logs piled high by the roadside or sinister branches lurking in her path.

"Get on with you, you idiot," Jinny shouted when for what seemed like the hundredth time her arm was nearly pulled out of its socket. "You can't be so lame if you can jump about like that." But whenever Shantih recovered from her fright she went back to her limping walk.

It had begun to rain; slow, steady rain that soaked Jinny's hair and seeped down her neck despite her up-turned collar. Her hands were numb with it and Shantih's reins slippery between her fingers. Totally depressed, Jinny plodded on. She had lost Kelly for a second time and although she couldn't see that it had been her fault this time she knew what her family would say.

Desperately Jinny hoped against hope that Kelly would have gone straight home. She tried to picture him lying in the kitchen or waiting forlornly on the front doorstep. But the only picture she could see was of an empty doorstep or a deserted kitchen. Even the thought of how well Shantih had jumped at the cross-country couldn't cheer her up. It didn't really matter. If she hadn't come to Miss Tuke's, Kelly wouldn't be lost and Shantih wouldn't be lame.

"Oh, why did Ken have to go away?" Jinny said aloud into the gathering dark, the words bursting out of her before she even knew she was going to say them. "Why? Why?"

It was black dark when Jinny at last reached home. Shapes of trees and Finmory House were only a denser black on blackness. For a split second Jinny forgot that Kelly had run away. For a warm, gulping moment she was standing in their safe, stone-flagged kitchen, telling her family how well Shantih had jumped, showing them the rosette, listening to their pleased surprise. But it was only for a moment, then cold reality was back. Kelly had gone.

All the way home Jinny had kept on calling him, trying to keep her voice welcoming, as if she knew he was just out of sight and would come rushing up to her when she called. But no grey, shaggy dog had come bounding to her.

"He could be anywhere, anything could be happening to him," Jinny thought. The terrible, dead despair of searching for a lost dog gripped at her heart.

"Kelly! Come on, Kelly," she called. "Kelly, Kelly." Tears pricked behind her eyes as she led Shantih into her box.

When Jinny had brushed Shantih down and fed her, she left her with her nose buried in her feed and went slowly up to the house to tell them that Kelly was lost again.

Jinny opened the back door and stepped into the kitchen. Her mother was working at the sink, her father and two men were sitting at the kitchen table. There was no sign of Kelly. Jinny stood blinking in the brightness as they all turned to stare at her.

"Here she is," said her father as Jinny shut the door and stepped into the kitchen. "Jinny, this is Mr. Hendry and Mr. Gault."

Jinny glowered suspiciously at the two men. They were obviously farmers, with weather-beaten faces and gnarled hands. She didn't recognise Mr. Gault, the younger man, but she had seen Mr. Hendry in Mr. MacKenzie's yard. He farmed Garthlarnock, a farm about ten miles away.

"They've come over to ask us about Kelly," her father continued as Jinny shut the door. "Apparently there has

73

been a grey dog chasing sheep on the moors. They seem to think it is Kelly. Mr. Hendry saw it this afternoon."

"Aye, no doubt to it," said Mr. Hendry. "The tyke belonging to that hippy who lives here. It's the only grey dog that size in these parts."

"Of course," said Mr. Manders, "we told him that it couldn't possibly be Kelly he'd seen, since he's been away with you all day. They've been waiting to see him."

Jinny felt the blood drain from her face. She stared at her father in dismay; felt her mother watching her, suspecting that something was wrong.

"He's . . . But . . ." stuttered Jinny.

"Let's see the brute," said the younger farmer impatiently. "You can tell by the look of them if they've taken to the sheep killing."

"Aye," agreed Mr. Hendry. "And once they start it a bullet's the only cure. I've shot one of my own dogs for it. She knew herself she'd been at the killing."

"Jinny," said her mother sharply, interrupting the farmer's story. "Go and get Kelly."

Blindly, Jinny turned and went back outside. She ran down the path to the stables, stood in the stable doorway holding on to the jamb of the door, staring out into the blackness. Inside she could hear Shantih, safe and secure, munching her oats, but Kelly was somewhere out there in the darkness, wandering, searching.

The farmer's words battered in Jinny's head, "a bullet's the only cure for it."

She would have to go back and tell them that Kelly had run away from Miss Tuke's, that she didn't know when he'd escaped and the farmers would be more certain than ever that it had been Kelly chasing their sheep.

"But it's not. He wouldn't kill sheep. He wouldn't. Kelly never, never looks at sheep. He only wants to find Ken." But Jinny knew that the farmers wouldn't listen to her.

"Kelly," she called into the night garden. "Kelly! Kelly! Kelly!"

Tears ran down her face. In a minute she would have to go back and tell them the truth.

"Kelly, Kelly come," she called despairingly.

There was no sound. Jinny rubbed her eyes on her jacket sleeve.

"If only Ken was here," she thought and shouted again, hopelessly, "Kelly! Kelly!"

From somewhere in the direction of the sea there was a rushing, scrabbling sound.

"Kelly!" screamed Jinny. "Come on. Kelly come."

There was a fluster of paws and Kelly came leaping and bounding out of the dark. He pushed against Jinny's legs, thrusting his wet nose and licking tongue into her hand.

"Oh, Kelly," Jinny cried, kneeling down and flinging her arms round his shaggy neck. "Where have you been? You dog, you bad, stupid dog."

Holding firmly on to Kelly's collar she marched him back into the house.

"Here he is," she said as she opened the kitchen door and let Kelly go. "He came to Miss Tuke's with me this morning and here he is back home. You couldn't have seen him on the moors."

The two farmers watched without smiling as Kelly wagged a welcome to Mr. and Mrs. Manders and then lay down on the floor.

"We'll away then," said Mr. Hendry. "And our apologies to you for troubling you on the Sabbath. Be keeping that dog under control now. There's sheep being killed on the hill and it's a grey dog that's doing it. No doubt to it."

"Keep him in the house," Mr. Gault said to Jinny, "for there's not a farmer that wouldn't be taking the gun to him if they saw him on the hill."

"Kelly wouldn't touch your sheep," declared Jinny. "Ask Mr. MacKenzie, he'll tell you."

But the two men were shaking hands with her father and paid no more attention to Jinny.

"Thank goodness they've gone," said Mrs. Manders when her husband came back after seeing the two farmers away. "Not the pleasantest company."

"Seems there's been at least six sheep killed," said Mr. Manders. "Even a dog chasing sheep at this time can harm the ewes."

"We know it isn't Kelly," said Mrs. Manders. "He's

been on the hills since we came here and he's never once looked at a sheep. You'd think they'd realise that and stop suspecting him."

Even when she was telling her family about her day at Miss Tuke's Jinny didn't mention anything about Kelly's escape. It seemed better if they didn't know.

Later that evening Jinny was brushing Kelly.

"Where did you go to?" she asked him as she tried to tug a comb through his mass of grey, shaggy hair.

"Now your other foot," she told him and started to brush out his paw. "You've got to stop this nonsense. No more running away. If one of those farmers saw you even crossing the moor . . ."

Jinny stopped in mid-sentence. Caught between the toes of Kelly's foot was a tuft of blood-stained sheep's wool. Although she knew the kitchen was empty Jinny glanced guiltily over her shoulder before she freed the wool from Kelly's claws, dashed across to the fire and threw it on to the flames.

CHAPTER EIGHT

"Can I come with you?" Mike asked, appearing at Shantih's box door as Jinny was grooming her the next Saturday morning.

"Course," said Jinny. "I'm going for a long ride to calm her down. She's jumping out of her skin doing nothing all week."

"Is she O.K. to ride now?" Mike asked.

"Yes," said Jinny. "Really she was sound on Wednesday but I thought I'd better give her the whole week off with no one riding her."

"Any longer and Dad would have been going round to Miss Tuke's himself for another trekking pony."

"Yes," agreed Jinny, thinking back over the past week when her father had had to drive her in and out to Glenbost every day. "He's light the blue touch paper and retire, in the mornings."

"I'll go and get Bramble then," Mike said and went.

Kelly was lying in the stable doorway. He lifted his head from his paws to watch Mike then dropped it back, whining to himself.

"Oh, Kelly, don't," Jinny called to him. "You're coming with us."

Kelly heard her voice and came pattering down to Shantih's box. His long grey nose appeared under the box door making Shantih peer, prick-eared, goggle-eyed then drift suddenly sideways, nearly knocking Jinny over.

Half an hour later they were mounted and riding up the track to the moors, Shantih leading the way. Her tail was kinked high over her quarters, her neck arched, her oiled hooves flirting dirt and stones as she pranced and fretted to be allowed to gallop. Bramble, bustling and hairy, bumbled along behind her with Mike riding bareback. Kelly trotted at Bramble's side, his grey, sickle tail wagging with delight, his sucker nose drawing in all the smells of the open moorland.

"Right for a canter?" Jinny called back.

"Right," replied Mike, digging his knees tighter into Bramble's sides.

Shantih knew the canter as well as Jinny. Hardly were the words out of Jinny's mouth than Shantih's head disappeared between her knees and her heels flew skywards in an enormous buck before she stretched herself out at a flying gallop. Sitting neat and tight, Jinny urged her on. The red ruin of the summer's bracken crackled under the Arab's pounding hooves, flakes of shimmering rock and peaty gravel were flung out behind her in soaring arcs as Shantih plunged over the moorland.

Jinny heard Bramble's hoofbeats fade behind her, yet, like a grey shadow, streamlined by his own speed, Kelly raced at their side. They seemed to gallop together on an arc of moorland like figures in an old-fashioned hunting print where the hounds and the horses were always shown with legs outstretched to their uttermost, in an attempt to show their speed.

Jinny's long hair was blown out behind her as she crouched close to Shantih, her knuckles pressed against Shantih's neck and her feet braced against her stirrups. All the problems of Inverburgh Comprehensive School had gone – the teachers, the homework, the mystery of the time-tables had all vanished as if they had never existed. Jinny laughed aloud for sheer joy of movement and delight in the flying speed of her horse. As they raced over the moor Jinny had forgotten everything except Shantih – had even forgotten the dull ache of Ken's absence.

"Whacky racers," said Mike when he caught up with Jinny again. "Is she as fast as a racehorse? Or does she just seem so fast compared to Bramble?"

"Don't know," said Jinny as she walked Shantih beside Bramble, considering the question. "I don't think she would be as fast as your actual racehorse. They're all fed up on fancy food. Expect that would make a difference."

"What about your actual Kelly hound? He kept up with you and he isn't even panting."

At the sound of his name Kelly looked up, his eyes bright, his tail waving.

"Bet he could cross these moors faster than any horse," went on Mike. "Bet Kelly would be like a jaguar. Fastest animal."

"Cheetah?" suggested Jinny.

"Well," agreed Mike.

"They're fastest for short bursts of speeds," said Jinny.

Jinny, changed the subject, asked if they still had the hermit crabs in Glenbost school. She didn't want to think too much about Kelly's speed, about how his long rangy legs and spring-heeled feet could carry him over the moors like rain.

Mike, Jinny and Kelly shared Jinny's bar of chocolate sitting on a rock by the side of Loch Varrich.

"D'you think the ospreys will come back?" Mike said, looking across to the clump of pine trees where the ospreys had nested in the spring.

"Ken says they will."

"Odd the way he's never written. For all we know he may be anywhere. May not be in Amsterdam at all. You'd think he would have written us one letter."

"Be warned," said Jinny. "You sound like Petra. Next thing you'll be saying he *should* have written."

"Should have written one letter," insisted Mike. "Have you written to him?"

"Nope. I want to write to him and tell him about Kelly being so miserable but it would really be me telling him I want him back and using Kelly as an excuse."

"It's so flat without him," agreed Mike. "Couldn't you write?"

"It would only make him mad," Jinny said, standing up and shaking back her hair. "Let's go on a bit further."

Mike scrambled back on to Bramble. "Do you know Peter Farson?" he asked as they rode along. "That fat boy with red hair. Well, he's a super goalie. He can stop anything, jump miles into the air. You can't get a ball past him . . ."

Jinny listened with half an ear to Mike's story of how Peter had saved the match for Glenbost the last time they played Ardtallon. The rest of her was thinking about Kelly. As far as she could gather from Mr. MacKenzie, without sounding too concerned about it, the grey dog was still worrying the sheep.

"It's a nasty business," Mr. MacKenzie had said grimly. "They'll be taking to the hills with their guns and I'm for telling you that when that happens you'd best be having that Kelly shut up with the windows barred, for there's plenty of them are saying there's no doubt but that it's him with the killer cunning on him to hide it from you."

"You weren't listening," accused Mike, coming to the end of his story.

"Was," said Jinny. "Pretty good saving all those goals. Shall we find a place to jump?"

Mike agreed and they left the loch, riding over the moor alongside a dry stone wall, searching for a suitable place to jump it.

"What's that?" demanded Mike, pointing to a whiteish heap of something lying on the other side of the wall.

Jinny had seen it at the same moment. She stood up in her stirrups to see it better. There were dark red patches on the white.

"Don't know," she said and urged Shantih closer.

"It's . . ." began Mike, then stopped, and they both stared in horror at the dead sheep lying by the wall. For a

79

second they were held in a frozen silence, both afraid to speak. The only sound was Kelly whimpering in a high-pitched whine.

Jinny thought she was going to be sick. She slid down from Shantih so that she couldn't see the sheep but she could still smell its stench. She buried her face in Shantih's mane but the dead sheep was there as vividly as if her eyes had been open – the blue, scummed eyes glazed and solid, its throat torn open, the blood staining the dirty wool and a bloody hole where its guts had been torn out.

Kelly's whine became louder and more excited. Jinny opened her eyes again and in one sure grab had him by the collar. She was certain that he had been about to spring over the wall.

"Let's get away," she shouted to Mike and still, clutching Kelly's collar, Jinny led Shantih back to the loch side.

Jinny couldn't stop shaking, her teeth chattered and her hand holding Kelly shook uncontrollably.

"But it couldn't have been Kelly," Mike said, staring anxiously at his sister.

"I know it couldn't," said Jinny. "I know but the farmers don't. That Mr. Hendry *saw* a grey dog chasing his sheep last Sunday."

"That couldn't have been Kelly. He was with you at Miss Tukes."

"Kelly ran off from Miss Tuke's," admitted Jinny. "Miss Tuke has only to mention it and they'll know I was covering up for him. He's been on the moors this week too. Mum said how pleased she was that he's stopped moping and has been out and about again."

"But he's never chased sheep before and we'd have seen the blood on him."

"The other night he'd blood-stained wool caught between his claws," said Jinny.

"Go on," said Mike scornfully. "He often has scraps of wool caught on him. Bet you couldn't be sure it was blood. You'd be so worked up that peat or mud even would look like blood to you."

"Mr. MacKenzie says they clean themselves before they

come home, roll in a bog or swim. We'd never have noticed that. He's often wet and muddy."

"You don't think it could be him?" said Mike, looking at Kelly as he stood with his hackles raised, still whining with the high-pitched, nerve-searing note.

"Of course I don't think it's him. Kelly would never, ever kill anything."

Jinny pulled the length of binder twine out of her pocket and tied it securely round Kelly's collar.

"We've got to get home," she said. "As quickly as we can. We've got to make a kennel for him. Somewhere he can't get out of, where he can stay all day. Then no matter what they say they can't take him, for we'll have proof that it can't be him. He can't be in two places at once and we'll know that he's been at Finmory all day."

Jinny sprang back on to Shantih.

"Come on," she said. "We've got to have it finished for tonight. Then he can get used to it while I'm here to watch him."

Jinny wasn't much use with hammers and nails and wood. She could see in her mind's eye how the thing she wanted to make would look when it was finished, but after the nails kept on bending when she tried to hammer them in and she had failed to saw through even the thinnest piece of wood, she usually gave up in disgust.

"You're much better at it than me," she said to Mike after lunch. "I'll do what you tell me. Like fetching things or holding them. It's no good me building it. It's got to be solid. Strong enough so that he can't possibly get out."

Kelly was tied securely to the stable door while Jinny and Mike surveyed the end stall.

"We'll need to have a door to shut him in," said Jinny. "And wire netting or something to stop him jumping over into the other stall and getting out that way."

Mike looked dubiously at the stall. There seemed an awful lot of space to be filled in if it was going to be made escape-proof.

"Let's get started," urged Jinny. "I've brought Dad's tools. We'll need to scratch around for wood and netting."

They scratched around without much success. When they carried their findings back to the stable even the roll

81

of rusty wire-netting which was their best find wasn't anything like enough to turn the stall into a kennel.

"We'll never manage it," said Mike. "We haven't anything like enough and I don't really know what to do."

"Of course you do," snapped Jinny. "It's simple."

"Then do it yourself," said Mike.

Mr. Manders, hearing their raised voices, came into the stable to discover what they were doing.

"We're converting," said Jinny, liking the word. "Turning Punch's stall into a kennel for Kelly."

"But he's never needed a kennel before," said Mr. Manders, regarding their pieces of rotting wood and rusty netting with less than enthusiasm. "He's been so much better this week. Back to normal. Out on the hills."

"He's got to be shut in during the day when I'm not here to be with him," stated Jinny.

"Where did you get this notion from?" asked her father.

"Because of the sheep," said Jinny. "We've got to be able to prove that Kelly has been here all day; that he couldn't have been near the sheep."

"We found a dead sheep on the moors this morning," explained Mike. "It had its throat torn open and its insides eaten. A dog must have killed it."

"Whee!" exclaimed Mr. Manders, whistling his breath through his teeth. "Near here?"

"Loch Varrich," said Mike.

"Near enough," agreed Mr. Manders. "That puts a different aspect on it. Let's get going. You want to close this stall in so that Kelly can be left here through the day, that the idea? Let's see now, what would be the best way of doing it."

Even with their father working with them they weren't finished until Sunday afternoon.

"Well, that seems to be it," Mr. Manders said when the last nail had been knocked into place. "Alcatraz. He won't escape from there."

They had fixed wooden bars between the stalls and over half the doorway. For the bottom half of the doorway Mr. Manders had made a wire-netting frame that was

82

held in place by two planks resting on hooks screwed to the sides of the stall.

"Let's see how he likes it," suggested Mr. Manders.

"He won't," said Jinny. "He'll hate it, but better bored than shot."

Jinny led Kelly into his kennel and left him there, telling him to stay.

"Poor old boy," said Mr. Manders.

"He's not," said Jinny, hardening her heart against Kelly's wistful eyes gazing out at her from under his thatch of hair. "You stay there and you'll be safe."

"And it'll be the only place for him, I'm thinking," said a voice from the yard.

They all sprang round to see Mr. MacKenzie standing there. Not the farmer they were used to, but a severe, God-fearing man, straight-laced into his Sabbath suit and black tie.

"Mr. MacKenzie!" exclaimed Jinny in astonishment, for the farmer hardly ever came up to Finmory and never in his Sunday clothes.

"Good day to you," he said.

"Good afternoon," said Mr. Manders, walking out of the stable. "Can I help you?"

"It's the grey day," replied the farmer, avoiding the direct question. "It's building the ark you'll be at next if this rain keeps on."

"Might be a good idea," agreed Mr. Manders. "Though I think that will do me for the time being. I miss Ken for this kind of thing."

"I'm thinking it's a bit pity altogether that the lad had to go. Settling in fine he was and yourselves not hearing from him."

Mr. MacKenzie paused to spit sympathetically over his shoulder and then came to the point of his visit.

"There'd have been no trouble with the dog if he'd been here to keep an eye on him. That's what's started the poor brute to the killing."

Jinny scowled up furiously at Mr. MacKenzie. She had been fairly sure when she had seen him that he had come about Kelly.

"What do you mean?" she demanded indignantly. "Kelly hasn't been near any sheep."

Mr. MacKenzie ignored her and went on speaking to Mr. Manders.

"You'd Jock Hendry and the lad Gault over seeing you the other night. I'm knowing because they were dropping in for the word with me after they'd seen you. Jock had seen Kelly after his sheep that day, but with it being the Sabbath his gun was in the house. Now you were telling him that Kelly had been at Miss Tuke's for the whole day so it couldn't have been him Jock had seen. Well, I'd the wee word with Miss Tuke myself and it seems the dog escaped from her place in the morning."

Jinny felt herself blush scarlet.

"Is that right?" Mr. Manders asked, but he didn't need an answer. One glance at his daughter's face told him that Jinny had been lying.

"But he came back here," said Jinny. "He wasn't near the sheep."

"I'm thinking he had the good opportunity and it's Jack Hendry's eyes I'll be trusting, not your tongue."

"It's a very nasty business," said Mr. Manders. "But I can promise you that there'll be no more trouble from him."

"There hasn't been any trouble," interrupted Jinny. "Kelly wouldn't kill a sheep. He wouldn't kill anything."

"We shan't let him out of our sight from now on. When he's not with one of us he'll be shut in there."

Mr. MacKenzie looked unconvinced.

"Then I'll be hoping you'll manage it," he said. "It's not an easy thing to be keeping them in once they take to killing."

"I've told you, Kelly has never killed anything," stormed Jinny.

"And I'm here to be telling you that if I see the dog on my hill or in my yard I'll be shooting him myself."

For seconds not one spoke. Even Mr. Manders was shocked.

"You can't. You can't do that," cried Jinny. "Kelly knows your yard. He's used to going there. He couldn't do any harm if he was only in your yard."

But Mr. MacKenzie had already left them and was walking stiffly away.

"He means it," said Mike. "He would shoot Kelly. He really would."

It wasn't until that evening, when Jinny was standing in Shantih's box waiting for her to finish her evening feed, that the thought which had been itching at the back of Jinny's mind all day came into reach.

"Fact one," thought Jinny, ticking them off on her fingers. "That sheep have been killed." And her imagination jumped into nightmare flashes of sudden terror, the long-forgotten fear of the grey shape stalking through the heather to leap at the sheep's throat.

"Fact two," thought Jinny swiftly. "It was not Kelly."

"Fact three, there has been a grey dog on the moors, a strange grey dog that the farmers don't know."

Jinny held the three things in her mind, staring at Shantih yet not really seeing her, her eyes unfocused.

"But of course!" Jinny screamed aloud, making Shantih flinch and peer round curiously. "Of course! Why didn't I think of it before. It's not a dog. It's a wolf. One of Ralph Gilbert's wolves. There were six and then there were only five. One must have escaped and that's what the gamekeeper was searching for on our hill. It's a wolf that's killing the sheep. Not Kelly – one of Ralph Gilbert's wolves."

CHAPTER NINE

"You are dirty, untidy and totally irresponsible."

"Yes, Miss Brenner," said Jinny.

"I want none of your insolence. You'll go to detention tonight. Tell Mr. Wilkes that I sent you and he'll give you work to do."

Jinny said nothing, since agreeing seemed to annoy Miss Brenner and disagreeing certainly wouldn't please her.

Coming out from detention at four-thirty meant that Jinny had to catch the five o'clock bus to Glenbost, saddle

Shantih in the dark and ride home following the beam of her torch.

"Perhaps I could find some way of fixing my torch to the neckband of my martingale," Jinny thought as she waited for the bus after detention. "Probably fall off no matter what I did." She sighed aloud, making an old man who was standing next to her in the bus queue tell her that she had nothing to worry about at her age and to wait until she was as old as he was before she started sighing like that.

"Little does he know," thought Jinny. All the time, every minute of the day she was thinking about Kelly shut up in his kennel, gazing hopelessly between the bars, whining to be let out whenever he heard footsteps. "But better than being shot," Jinny had to keep reminding herself. She kept on wondering what Ken would have done if he'd been here, and what he would say if he knew that Kelly was being shut up all day.

When Jinny had told her family that she was certain it was one of Ralph Gilbert's wolves that had escaped from its enclosure and was living on the moors killing the sheep, they hadn't taken her seriously. Her father had been more inclined to return to the topic of how wrong it was to act a lie even if you didn't actually speak it. Petra, packing up for her return to her school hostel on Monday morning, had kept on humming "Who's afraid of the big, bad wolf?"

When Jinny arrived at Glenbost, Shantih was waiting by the gate of her field, her ears pinned back and her tail twitching, cross at being kept waiting.

"I know, I know. You should have been fed by now. I'm sorry but it's not my fault. I'm cross and starved and fed up too."

Shantih's soft muzzle pushed at Jinny's pocket, searching for titbits.

"Sorry," said Jinny, fishing out a peppermint. "Honest it wasn't my fault. We'll soon be home now."

By the light of her torch Jinny saddled up, and, leading Shantih out of the field, she mounted and began to ride home. Jinny knew the road to Finmory so well that she hardly needed the bobbing light of her torch. Shantih was anxious to get home and trotted out at a steady pace, going well into her bit, the regular sound of her hooves the only noise in the silent night.

"Soon be home," Jinny told her and felt the warm glow of coming home spread over her. The lights of Finmory shone through the bare branches of the trees, golden and welcoming.

When Jinny reached the stables, the door of Kelly's kennel was open and she supposed that he must be inside with the rest of the family.

After feeding Shantih, Jinny led her out to her field. Her white stockings glinted in the dark, her white face was like a lamp uplifted and Jinny could just make out her eyes glistening as she searched the darkness for Bramble.

Jinny opened the gate and led Shantih through as Bramble came looming up, nostrils flurrying a welcome. Jinny rubbed her hand through Bramble's dense coat, gave both horses a sugarlump then waited as they wandered off to graze.

Jinny walked into the kitchen, the grey hearthrug of Kelly came wagging and stretching to meet her and Jinny felt the tight knot in the pit of her stomach unclench itself. Kelly was safe.

"Has he been O.K.?" she demanded.

"Where have you been?" asked her mother. "Not detention again?"

Mike was homeworking at a corner of the table, her father was reading and her mother taking buns from a baking sheet and putting them on a tray to cool.

"Cheese?" asked Jinny hopefully.

"Yes," said her mother. "For you."

"Delish," said Jinny.

"Where have you been?" asked her mother again.

"Detention," said Jinny. "Has Kelly been all right?"

"I took him for a walk this morning and that settled him for his afternoon lock-in," said her father.

"Good," said Jinny, scratching Kelly behind his ears. "Did you enjoy it? You won't have to be shut in much longer. Just until they find the wolf and know it's not you."

"It must be a most fantastical experience living inside your head," her mother said, putting down a plate of kept-hot dinner.

"It is," agreed Jinny sitting down at the table as there was a sound of cars in the drive.

Kelly sprang to his feet, ready to bark, and Mr. Manders got up.

"Wonder who that can be," he said as the cars stopped at the front door.

They heard car doors opening and shutting and then the front door bell. Mr. Manders went to answer it.

Jinny heard men's voices and the tramp of their feet as they followed her father through to the kitchen. Instantly, she thought, "Kelly," and wondered if they had heard that he had escaped from Miss Tuke's.

Mr. Manders stood back, letting in Mr. Gault and Mr. Hendry, the two farmers who had been there before, and behind them a policeman.

"Good evening," said the policeman, a lard-faced, stolid figure, speaking to Mrs. Manders. "It's sorry I am to be bursting in on you like this."

Jinny saw her father lift his eyebrows, signalling trouble to his wife, before he closed the door. She looked quickly at the farmers and saw that one of them was carrying a gun over his shoulder. Instinctively, Jinny gripped Kelly's collar and pulled him to her side.

"It would be better if the children left the room," said the policeman.

"No," said Mr. Manders. "They are in this as much as the rest of us."

"Well now, it's like this," said the policeman, rocking on his heels, not looking at anyone as he spoke. "You'll be knowing that sheep are being killed on the moors. Ten have been reported to me and we'll not be knowing yet how many more are dead. So you'll understand that it's a serious business."

"We've come for the dog," said Mr. Gault. "It should have been done the other Sunday but you sent us off with a pack of lies."

Jinny grabbed Kelly closer to her. She felt panic surging in her, her eyes flickered from the farmers to the policeman. Who were they to come bursting into Finmory? What did they mean they had come for the dog? They couldn't take Kelly away. He was in his own home and they couldn't touch him.

"If you were misled on Sunday I'm sorry about it," said Mr. Manders. "Kelly did run away from Miss Tuke's but he came straight back here. Since then he hasn't been away at all. We've built a kennel for him and he'll be kept in it until you find the real culprit."

"It certainly is not Kelly," said Mrs. Manders. "He's been here for two years and he hasn't looked at a sheep. Surely if he'd been a sheep-worrier he'd have shown it before now."

"That's no the way of it," said Mr. Hendry. "I've known dogs that have worked the sheep for years start to the killing, and you'll not break them from it. You'd best be giving him to us now. There's no other way for it."

"You have no proof that our dog has been killing sheep," said Mr. Manders. "Until you have proof there is nothing you can do."

"I have the proof of my own eyes," stated Mr. Hendry coldly. "I saw him running my sheep. That's proof enough for me. If it were a stray dog we'd have shot him by now, but this brute has a home to go to, somewhere to hide, and there's not another grey dog living in a house or a farm near here."

"Come on," said the younger farmer, standing up, slipping his gun from his shoulder. "Best be doing what we're here for." He stepped towards Kelly, stretching out his hand to take him from Jinny.

"Get out. Get away. Leave him," Jinny screamed. "You've no right to come here. Get out."

"Steady," warned her father, but he came across and stood between Jinny and the farmer. "Be quite clear on this," he said. "Under no circumstances will I allow you to shoot my dog. Please sit down again."

For a moment the farmer faced up to Mr. Manders and Jinny thought he was going to push her father out of the way and try to take Kelly, who was pulling against Jinny's hold on his collar, growling and snarling in his throat.

"Enough, enough now," said Mr. Hendry. "I was saying

from the start we should have had the children out of the room. You'll not be understanding our ways, Mr. Manders, coming from the city. A ewe in lamb is worth a good deal of money. Now you wouldn't be having a man stealing from you and you be doing nothing to stop him, would you now? It's understood amongst us that when a dog turns sheep-killer we deal with it this way. We shoot him. It has to happen in the end so it's easier for us all if we do it now."

"No," shouted Jinny. "No! It's not Kelly that's killing your sheep. It's a wolf." And to her infuriated dismay she saw all the adults turn and look at each other with identical expressions of disbelief on their faces.

"It's true! Ralph Gilbert had six wolves. I saw them. Then the next week there were only five. One had escaped. I saw the gamekeeper searching for it on the moors. And that's when the killings started. It's a wolf, I tell you. It's a wolf that's killing your sheep."

"Oh, Jinny," said her mother.

"It's the powerful imagination she has on her," said Mr. Hendry incredulously.

"You must know that Ralph Gilbert keeps wolves," cried Jinny, turning to the policeman. "It's the kind of thing the police must know about."

"Well now," said the policeman. "I'd better not be sending my grandmother to find out."

Jinny realised that it was impossible. They weren't going to believe her, weren't even going to listen to her seriously and she couldn't make them. She scowled round at them, gripping Kelly's collar in both hands.

"Now, Mr. Manders," said the policeman, "do you agree to have the dog put down or to let us shoot him?"

"No," said Mr. Manders. "In my view there is not enough evidence against him. But I will agree to keep him shut in his kennel until you've got the killer."

"Now I'm afraid, sir, that will not be good enough. If you won't agree to have him put down, the only alternative is for me to take him to the police station. I'll keep him there for a week. If there is another dog that's at the killing he'll be going on with it while Kelly is with me."

"Is that the choice?" Mr. Manders asked him.

90

"It is, it is. If you're not for giving him to me tonight I'll be back in the morning with the official documents to allow me to take him."

"Then he'd better go with you now," decided Mr. Manders.

"No," screamed Jinny. "You're not touching him!" She looked wildly round the room for a way of escape but she was too far from either door to be able to reach it without being stopped.

"He's got to go," said her father, coming to take Kelly from her. "Nothing can happen to him while he's with the police."

"Anything could happen," cried Jinny, holding on grimly to Kelly's collar. "They could let the farmers shoot him and say it was an accident. They could have him destroyed and tell us he'd run away. They mustn't have him. They can't take him."

Mr. Manders loosened Jinny's fingers from Kelly's collar.

"Now don't make a scene," he said.

Jinny was beyond listening. She struck out blindly with her clenched fist. "Leave him alone," she cried.

Mr. Manders fended her off and forced her to let go of Kelly. He dragged the dog across to the policeman, who took a chain out of his pocket and clipped it on to Kelly's collar.

Jinny launched herself at him, kicking and scratching as she fought to make him let go of Kelly. Mr. Manders pulled Jinny away and wrapping his arm round her held her against his side, unable to move.

"If the dog is hurt in any way," Mr. Manders said, "there will be serious trouble. No one is certain that he is the dog who has been killing the sheep. The only reason I'm letting you take him with you tonight is to prove to you that sheep will go on being killed while Kelly is shut up."

"Don't be worrying now," said the policeman. "We'll be sorting it out. No harm will come to the dog while we have him. He's safer in our kennels than here, where there's not a farmer but would shoot him on sight."

Mrs. Manders took them to the front door, the police-
91

man dragging Kelly, his legs splayed, his claws scrabbling as he fought to stay with Jinny.

Mr. Manders didn't let go of his daughter until he heard the cars driving away.

"It's the only way," he told her as she threw herself into a chair, tears pouring down her face. "It is true what the policeman said. Kelly is safer at the police station. When they have him there and the sheep are still being killed they'll know it can't be Kelly. If we'd kept him here they'd never have believed us. They'd have thought he was getting out without us knowing."

But Jinny wasn't listening to reason. She glared up balefully at her father.

"You let them take him," she said. "He could still be here. We could have kept him until tomorrow morning but you let them take him."

"If Kelly had stayed here tonight you'd have found some way of trying to hide him and that would have been the worst thing you could possibly have done. As bad as saying it was him."

Jinny pushed herself up out of the chair. "I hate you all," she shouted and dashed out of the kitchen up to her bedroom.

"Now stop crying," she told herself. "They've got Kelly and those farmers want to shoot him. They don't care about policemen. All they want is to see Kelly dead. I've got to stop them. I've got to let Ken know what's happened."

Jinny found paper and sat down to write.

"Dear Ken,

I have to write to you. The farmers here think that Kelly has been killing their sheep. Of course it has not been him. Tonight two of them came here with a policeman. They wanted to shoot Kelly."

Staring at the words, Jinny could still hardly believe that it could be true. People didn't arrive and want to shoot your dog. It wasn't possible. It couldn't really happen. But it had.

"They have taken him to the police station. I couldn't stop them."

Jinny thought of different ways of saying "come back at

once" without it sounding like that but in the end she only wrote, *"love Jinny."*

If he doesn't come when he knows that they might shoot Kelly there's no point in asking him to come, she decided, and put the letter in an envelope. Then she realised that she didn't know Ken's address.

"There was a catalogue for that pottery exhibition," Jinny thought. "It gave the names and addresses of all the potters who were exhibiting things. Bob Shultz's address will be in it."

Moving as quietly as she could, Jinny went down to her father's pottery to look for the catalogue. She found it without much trouble, looked up the index and turned to the page on Bob Shultz's pottery. It gave his name, address and telephone number. Jinny stare at it, mesmerized. A phone number meant you could phone the person, could lift up the phone, dial numbers and speak to them. It meant that Jinny could speak to Ken.

There was an extension phone in the pottery. No one would hear her. Jinny hesitated, crossed over and stood beside it. If she could speak to Ken and tell him what had happened to Kelly he would come back. He would have to come. He couldn't do anything else, not when he knew that they had taken Kelly away.

Jinny picked up the receiver. She dialled Directory Enquiries, asked the efficient voice how she would phone a number in Amsterdam and the voice told her the code to dial.

The dialling tone purred in her ear again. Jinny swallowed hard, bit her bottom lip, listened for any sound of her family and began to dial. There was a crackling of lines, then the phone ringing out in Bob Schultz's pottery in Amsterdam.

"Maybe Ken will hear it. Is hearing it," thought Jinny. "Maybe he'll answer it."

A man's voice answered, speaking in Dutch, for seconds Jinny was taken by surprise. She had never thought of them speaking anything but English.

"Hullo," she said, pulling herself together. "I want to speak to Ken Dawson."

"Are you English?" asked the voice.

93

"Yes," said Jinny. "I can't speak Dutch."

"Does not matter. I speak English."

"Can I speak to Ken?" demanded Jinny urgently. There was the sound of pop music and people laughing and talking in the background. It sounded to Jinny as if they were having a party. "Ken. Ken Dawson," she repeated.

"Hold the line. I shall try to find him."

"Tell him Jinny wants to speak to him. Tell him his dog is going to be shot; that the police have taken him away."

"I will tell him. Hold on."

Jinny waited, curled into herself. "He must come back. He must." The party noise swirled through her head. "Hurry up. Oh do hurry up."

"Hullo," said the voice that was not Ken.

"Yes?" said Jinny.

"He cannot come now."

"But did you tell him. Tell him about his dog."

"I gave him the message but Ken cannot speak now. Goodbye."

"I must . . ." But the phone clicked and was dead.

Numbly Jinny replaced the receiver. She went slowly back to her room and tore up the letter she had written to Ken. When he knew that Kelly might be shot and he hadn't even bothered to come to the phone there was no point in writing to him.

CHAPTER TEN

Jinny hardly slept all night. She got up at five o'clock, left a note on the kitchen table telling her mother where she had gone and rode to Glenbost, left Shantih in her field and hitched a lift to the police station at Ardtallon from a forestry worker who was a friend of Mr. MacKenzie's.

The policeman stuck his head out of an upstairs window in reply to Jinny's urgent ringing. It was the same man that had taken Kelly away.

"And what would you be after at this time in the morning?" he demanded.

"I've come to see Kelly," Jinny shouted back.

"It's yourself," he shouted back, recognising her. "Be off with you."

"I've to catch the school bus and I've got to see Kelly first," Jinny told him and went on ringing the bell until the policeman opened the door.

"I am sorry for troubling you," Jinny said, "but I must see him. Think what you'd be feeling if you were Kelly. A crowd of gunmen coming into your home and dragging you off. How would you like it? So I've got to see him." Jinny stared up at the policeman, all her will and mind and imagination totally fixed on being allowed to see Kelly.

"Now I'll be having none of this nonsense," began the policeman.

Jinny continued to stare straight at him, her face a blank mask of certainty. She had come to see Kelly and that was all there was to it. She would stand there ringing the door bell until he let her in.

"You've no business here at this hour. Be off home with you." But the policeman, faced with Jinny's stony expression, felt his anger at being disturbed start to fade. It was easy to see that Jinny had been crying and clear that she didn't intend to take no for an answer.

"I'd be needing to lock you in," said the policeman, weakening. "I can't be risking you taking him off."

Jinny had been hoping that the policeman would leave Kelly's door unlocked but there was nothing she could do about it just now. Perhaps as she went on visiting Kelly they'd get used to her and forget to lock the door.

"It doesn't matter," said Jinny, "as long as I can see him."

"Come on in with you then." The policeman took Jinny through the police office, past two human cells, to a smaller cell with a barred door. Kelly lay sprawled on a blanket put down on the tiles. He was fast asleep.

"Kelly," Jinny called and he sprang up, saw her, and came dashing towards her, sticking his head through the bars, whining and crying, his tail whirling in mad circles of delight.

The policeman unlocked the door and Jinny squeezed

through. Kelly wrapped his paws round her neck, his tongue licking her face in hot, wet sweeps. Jinny threw her arms round him, turning her back on the policeman.

"You can have half an hour and then it's your bus will be coming."

"O.K.," sniffed Jinny, hearing the door being locked behind her.

Jinny crouched down on the floor, opened her school bag and took out a flask of coffee and three rounds of buttered toast.

"Your favourite breakfast," she told Kelly, sharing the toast with him and blowing on the flask-top of coffee until it was cool enough for him to drink. "Now don't worry, because I'll sort things out somehow. I've thought about it all night and what I'm going to do is find where the wolf has its lair, where it's hiding. Then they'll know there is a wolf and that it's not you who is killing their sheep."

Kelly listened, his head on one side, his eyes fixed on Jinny's face.

"I can't get you out of here just now, but when I can I will. I'll be back this afternoon. I'll tell them at school that I've got a headache. Tomorrow I'm not going to school but I can't spend all day with you. I'll need to search for the wolf."

When the policeman came to let Jinny out she couldn't bear to leave Kelly. He was glued to her side, staring up at her with beseeching eyes.

"If you're not coming this instant," said the policeman, "you'll not be seeing that bus today. Come on with you now. There's no harm will come to the dog. Don't be upsetting yourself like this. Have a mind to all the poor sheep he's killed."

Jinny gave Kelly the biscuits she had brought for him and marched out of the cell.

"Kelly has not killed any sheep," she told the policeman as she walked away, hearing Kelly whining and scratching at the bars of his cage. "I've told you it's the wolf who's killing them."

Dolina was surprised to see Jinny getting on the bus at Ardtallon.

"I've been to see Kelly," Jinny said, and explained what had happened.

"Och, I've heard the talk of it," said Dolina. "The poor dog's safer in the police station than anywhere else. There's not one of them wouldn't shoot him if they had the chance. They go desperate wild when it's their sheep that are being killed."

"I'm sure it's a wolf that's killing the sheep," said Jinny, hoping beyond hope that at least Dolina would believe her.

"It's the good job," said Dolina, "that you're quick at the painting or they'd be shutting you up too. They don't mind you being mad when you've the artistic touch."

After her school dinner Jinny went to look for Miss Lorimer, the guidance teacher. After two trots down wrong corridors Jinny found her room. She knocked on the door.

"Come in," called Miss Lorimer and smiled at Jinny as she entered. "Can I help?" she asked, clearing papers off a chair so that Jinny could sit down.

"I've got a sore throat and a headache," said Jinny. "I'll need to go home."

"You certainly don't look too good," said Miss Lorimer sympathetically. "What's your name?"

"Jinny Manders."

"Ah yes, I've heard about you. You ride part of the way to school, don't you? Hope it isn't going to be too much for you, especially in the winter. I should think the best thing would be to go straight home and into bed. Can you get a bus about now?"

"There's one at two o'clock," said Jinny, feeling more guilty than ever when Miss Lorimer was being so understanding.

"Good. On you go then. I'll let your afternoon teachers know where you are."

"Thank you," said Jinny, meaning it, and hurried out of the room. She collected her school bag and coat, changed out of her skirt into her jodhs, and, thinking hard about Kelly, she marched out of school to catch the bus.

Jinny stayed on the bus until Ardtallon.

D

"I've come to see Kelly again," she said to the policeman.

"Well, you'll not be seeing him here, he's gone."

"What do you mean?" Jinny cried. "How has he gone?"

"Gone," repeated the policeman. "My wife took his food into him this morning, she was bending down speaking to him when the next minute he's out of the cell, through here like greased lightning and out of that door before one of us could stop him."

Jinny didn't know whether to be pleased or not. A bit of her couldn't help being glad that Kelly had escaped from the miserable cell, that he was free again, but the reasonable, commonsense part of Jinny knew that he would have been safer in the police station than running on the hills.

"It's the sorry day's work, I'm telling you. When the farmers hear he's loose again there'll be no stopping them this time."

Jinny hitched a lift back to Glenbost and tacked up Shantih, telling her what had happened. "So we've got to find out where the wolf is. We've got to find it before they shoot Kelly," she finished, leading Shantih out of the field and climbing into the saddle.

"You're home early today," Mrs. Simpson called from her shop doorway.

"Yes," said Jinny. "You're right I am."

"You'll have heard that dog of yours is loose among the sheep again?"

"Yes," said Jinny, wondering how people in Glenbost always knew about things almost before they happened.

"It wouldn't be yourself that arranged it, being so early out of the school?"

"No," said Jinny. "I had nothing to do with it."

"He should have been shot last night. Jock Hendry was telling me . . ." But Jinny was out of earshot.

Half way to Finmory, Jinny left the road and went over the moors. Once out of sight of the road she relaxed. Her parents weren't likely to see her now, although they were bound to find out that she had been at the police station and in the village when she should have been at school.

"Can't be helped," Jinny thought, and turned Shantih in the direction of Loch Varrich.

As Jinny rode, her eyes were skinned for every movement on the moorland that unrolled, wave upon wave, about her. When a sheep moved suddenly or a hoodie crow launched itself from a rock, Jinny's eyes searched for a grey shape. High above her an eagle hung in the sky, a dark, unmoving speck. "It can see us all," Jinny thought. "It can see where the wolf is. It sees us all like a map spread out below it."

A farmer Jinny didn't know crossed the moor, looking about him as he went. He was carrying a gun.

"He's looking for the wolf too," Jinny thought, then knew she was wrong. It was Kelly he was looking for, and by now Kelly might be back on the Finmory moors. Jinny shivered and urged Shantih into a trot.

She searched the moors all afternoon but she saw no sign of the wolf. The dead sheep was still lying by the wall at Loch Varrich. Jinny viewed it downwind. It looked much the same to her as it had last weekend which meant that the wolf hadn't been back to its kill.

"Perhaps it isn't anywhere near here," Jinny thought despondently as she rode on. It could have gone back to the hills around Bendarroch but Jinny didn't think it was likely. All the land around Bendarroch was planted with forestry pine trees. Where there were dense forestry plantations all other forms of life were dead. Around Finmory, the open moorland was grazed by black-faced sheep. "A wolf's supermarket," Jinny thought without even smiling.

She rode on beyond Loch Varrich and the light began to fade from the sky. The bracken glowed and the grey rocks seemed to give back the light they had stored during the day. Jinny knew it was time to turn back. She knew how quickly these luminous moments were followed by the dark.

"I'm mad," she thought. "What good am I doing here? If I saw the wolf I wouldn't know what to do about it."

Jinny brought Shantih to a halt. In every direction there was nothing to be seen but the desert of moor – rocks, dried bracken, dead, knotted heather and the close-cropped moorland grass. Somewhere in this wilderness the

wolf waited for the dark and somewhere on the moors
Kelly wandered, lost and alone, trusting no one, for now
all the humans that he had known had betrayed him.

Jinny turned Shantih and began to ride back to
Finmory. The night seemed to unroll from the mountains,
flowing down behind them, an unseen presence forcing
her to go faster as she felt its breath on the back of her
neck. The going was too rough for Shantih to do more
than walk but the Arab felt the coming dark. She jogged
against her bit, moving in sudden jerks and lunges as her
hooves slipped and stumbled.

Digging her knees in tight, Jinny gave Shantih her head,
doing nothing to slow her down. In the afternoon Jinny
had been the hunter, now, as the shadows became lapping
pools of darkness and the emerald scum on the peat bogs
gleamed with an eerie brilliance, Jinny was the hunted. No
longer was she searching for the wolf, she was escaping
from it. The terrors of the moors by night swarmed in
Jinny's imagination, all the moments from horror movies
when she hadn't shut her eyes were on the edge of being
remembered.

They were almost in sight of Finmory, following a track
through bracken that reached to Shantih's shoulder, when
Jinny became aware that there was something following
them; something alive in the bracken that moved when
they did, stood still waiting, watching when Jinny halted
Shantih and stood listening. Jinny let Shantih walk on
again, her ears peeled for the sounds that echoed her own
movements. It was there again, too certain for the random
scuttlings of rabbits, too heavy for the brisk patter of a
fox. The thing was listening and waiting for her.

Could a wolf attack a horse? Jinny didn't know. Could
it spring up and pull her from the saddle. Anything was
possible. Jinny's throat was tight with fear.

The bracken gave way to more open moorland, peaty
and broken, with the bones of rock breaking through the
surface. Jinny knew it would be too dangerous to risk
trotting in this light. She glanced quickly behind her and
saw a grey shape move, slinking, close to the ground.

For minutes that seemed like hours Jinny rode, frozen
with terror. To scream was useless for there was no one

to hear her, to gallop was to risk bringing Shantih down. There was nothing Jinny could do except to ride on as quickly as she dared over the treacherous ground. Once they reached the bottom of the slope there was a flat stretch of moorland where they could gallop. Would Shantih be faster than a wolf? Jinny had no idea. She could hear the wolf moving behind her, the scatter of stones when it leapt to keep up with her.

They had almost reached the foot of the slope before Jinny's imagination cooled down enough to allow a little commonsense to get into her head.

"If it is the wolf, why isn't Shantih upset?" she thought. "Shantih knows it's there. She must be able to see it and smell it yet she was paying no attention to it. Was it . . . Could it be . . ."

Jinny forced herself to turn round and look again. Kelly was trotting behind them.

"Kelly!" Jinny cried, relief, delight and the feeling of having been a total idiot, all mixed up in her voice. "Oh, Kelly, it's you! It's you!"

The dog came bounding up, his tail wagging, paws flopping, his eyes bright.

"Oh, dear Kelly," Jinny cried and flung herself down from Shantih.

When Jinny's feet touched the ground Kelly jumped back. He stood some distance away from Jinny. His tail was still wagging and his front paws beat a welcome on the ground.

"It's all right," said Jinny. "Come on, Kelly." She held her hand out, walking towards him.

Again the dog moved away, further this time. He sat down, still wagging and fussing, bright eyes fixed on Jinny.

"Kelly, come on, boy. It's all right. I'll not let them take you away again."

Kelly listened, his head on one side, whining to himself.

"There's a good boy. Come on, Kelly." Jinny stepped closer to him.

Kelly stood up, shook himself, barked once, then turned and trotted out of sight back to the moors.

CHAPTER ELEVEN

Jinny's parents were surprisingly understanding when she asked them if she could have Friday off school.

"I must find Kelly," Jinny said. "He could so easily be shot. I can't wait until Saturday."

She had decided not to mention searching for the wolf. Her parents were worried about Kelly but they still considered the wolf as a figment of Jinny's imagination.

"Please can I stay at home tomorrow and look for him?"

Mr. Manders considered the question. "If I agree and let you stay at home tomorrow to hunt for him, will you give me your word that if you don't find him you won't play truant next week to go looking for him?"

"Yes," said Jinny, "I promise."

Early on Friday morning she rode down through Mr. MacKenzie's yard, hoping to see him, for she was sure that if anyone might know where a wolf would hide on the moors it would be Mr. MacKenzie. It wasn't until she was riding away from the farm that Jinny saw him coming towards her, bringing three heifers down from the hill.

"So you've abandoned the book learning for the winter picnic," he said, stopping to lean on his stick as Jinny reached him.

"I'm going to look for Kelly."

"Aye, he's on the loose again. You'll not keep them in once they start to the killing."

From Shantih's back Jinny looked down at the farmer.

"Why won't you believe me?" she said. "Honestly, it isn't Kelly. It is a wolf."

"Will you be stopping such nonsense talk. I've a niece that cleans for Lady Gilbert when she's needing her and many's the tale I've heard her tell about Bendarroch. If there were any wolves prowling about the place I've the notion she'd have mentioned it before now."

"Well, I saw his animals. He had six wolves. Then the

next week there were only five. I'll bet you saw Mr. Paton on the moors. He'd two other men with him and they were looking for the wolf."

"Aye, he was asking me if he could be crossing the hill, but it was foxes they were after."

"That's what they'd tell you. They don't want anyone to know about them. I think they're scared anyone finds out."

Mr. MacKenzie stared at the ground, considering Jinny's ideas.

"If there'd been a wolf on the hills we'd have been seeing it," he said finally.

"But you have seen it. You've seen it and thought it was Kelly."

"No, no. The beast that's killing the sheep has a house to shelter him. If he was lying out on the open moor there'd be a bullet in him by now."

"Oh, why won't you listen?" cried Jinny in despair.

"It'll be the sorry day when the farmers round here have nothing better to do than listen to the likes of you with your blethers." And Mr. MacKenzie started off back down the hill.

He had only gone about a dozen steps when he stopped and waved his stick at Jinny, signalling to her to come back down to him.

"If it's a wolf you're set on finding, I'll tell you where I'd be looking. From the standing stones you can see three rowan trees growing in a wee circle. From the rowans you'll see the side of the hill facing you. Follow your nose to it. The hill there is riddled with caves. If your fairytale goings-on are true, I'm thinking that's where you'll find your wolf. Now away with you and leave me be."

"I'll go straight there and look," said Jinny. She hesitated, then added, "You wouldn't really shoot Kelly, would you? I'll find the wolf. I know I will and then you'll know it isn't him."

"Aye, fine," said Mr. MacKenzie as he stomped away.

Jinny went back to Finmory to get a halter. She put it on under Shantih's bridle. If she was going to be exploring caves she would need to tie Shantih up outside. Jinny also took her torch and a ball of garden twine, putting them into her rucksack with the other things that she had thought might come in handy.

It was a grey, moist, November day. The mountains and the further reaches of the moor were tones of pastel grey, fading into dimness. The sodden bracken was diamonded with moisture and the few leaves that still clung to the rowans and the birches were a transparent gold.

As Jinny rode she searched the moor, but all was quiet. The sheep grazed contentedly, their fleeces gemmed with mist; a few crows watched Jinny pass without bothering to fly off, and when a flight of gulls wavered across the sky their wings flapped heavily as if they flew through dense air. Shantih, too, seemed to walk and trot more solemnly through the grey, moisturized landscape.

The standing stones loomed on the horizon, appearing like vast gods towering out of the deserted moorland.

Jinny rode into the circle of the stones, dwarfed by their presence. She searched the moor for the rowans and saw them far ahead of her. She realised that the caves Mr. MacKenzie had meant must be in the hills that were no more than a smear of darker grey almost lost in the evanescent mists.

Not for a second did Jinny think of going back. The wolf was somewhere on the moors and she was there to find it. Jinny was vague about what would happen after she found the wolf. Would she tell the farmers so that they could shoot it? She didn't know. Hadn't thought as far ahead as that. She only knew that to find the wolf was the one way left to clear Kelly's name.

If Ken had been there he would have known what to do. Jinny thrust the thought of Ken out of her mind, battening it down where it couldn't reach her surface thoughts. Ever since Ken had refused to come to the phone Jinny had blocked him off, refused to think of him.

She closed her legs against Shantih's sides and the Arab walked out towards the rowan trees. The moor was flat here; a stretch of reaching marsh, speckled with clumps of dead, flaxen reeds and bald, sheep-cropped turf. As Jinny rode over the flat land she seemed to move in a trance of grey mist and charcoal shadows. Only her horse was real, walking out with a long, sure stride. Her white face and red-gold chestnut neck seemed to throb with rich colour in this leeched world.

When she reached the rowans Jinny didn't stop but rode on to where the far hillside, taking form and substance now, rose before her.

Jinny had no trouble in finding the caves Mr. Mac-Kenzie had told her about. One side of the hill was bare, grey rock; the openings to the caves were lipless, vertical mouths, varying in height from two feet to openings that stretched far above Jinny's head. Some were only inches across, others about three feet wide. It was easy to see why Mr. MacKenzie had thought this was where the wolf would have its lair.

Jinny slid down from Shantih and led her over to a gnarled hawthorn bush, more wind sculpture than tree. She took off her saddle and bridle and tied Shantih to a branch by her halter, then she tipped out a feed of pony nuts on to the grass.

"Stay there," Jinny said, throwing her arm over Shantih's withers, resting for a moment against the strong bulk of her horse. "Now don't be doing anything crazy."

Standing tied was not one of Shantih's favourite things, but Jinny hoped that nothing would disturb her and that she would be tired enough to want to stay where she was while she was alone.

Jinny took her torch and the ball of twine out of her rucksack and with one last look at Shantih she hurried across to the caves.

"Better work from left to right," she thought, hesitating at the entrance to the first cave.

"Jinny," she told herself severely, "get on with it now." And, switching on her torch, she walked into the first of the cave openings.

Water ran down the walls of the cave. Jinny flashed her torch and saw nothing but wet rock. No animal would choose to live in this cold wetness. She backed out and went on to the next opening. It, too, was damp and its walls covered with trickling water.

The next three caves were the same and Jinny was beginning to think that Mr. MacKenzie must be wrong.

"Maybe they've changed since he was here," she thought as she crouched down to shine her torch into a low cave opening. Inside something moved. Jinny's heart banged in her throat, she jumped back and a terrified rabbit burst out of the cave and zipped past her.

"Gosh," said Jinny, "fat lot of use I'd be if I did meet a wolf."

The fright with the rabbit woke Jinny up. She worked quickly, shining her torch over the walls and floors of the caves, checking for any signs of bones or dead animals which the wolf might have brought back to its lair.

When Jinny had looked into about twelve caves she came to the one that had the highest opening of all. She walked inside and shone her torch round walls and roof the size of a small room. It was quite dry. The walls were rough with overhangs and ledges. At the far end, a tunnel led off into the darkness. Jinny crossed the cave, shone her torch down the tunnel, and saw that it branched into two passages.

She stood for a moment, hesitating, and almost turned back, back to the daylight, the open moor and Shantih. "Jinny," she warned herself, "it's what you're here for. On you go."

Gritting her teeth, Jinny tied one end of her twine to a boulder at the mouth of the tunnel and, unwinding it behind her, she walked down the narrow passage. Her torch beam cast flickers of light but Jinny could feel the dark pressing in on her. Although she knew that the roof of the tunnel was at least two feet above her head, the second that Jinny couldn't see it she felt it closing in on her, was certain that it was creeping closer and closer. Jinny swung the torch in frantic circles. "Say I drop it," she thought. "Say it went out." A bird or a bat fluttered past her face and she screamed. Hundreds of echo screams vibrated around her.

Jinny stood, feet rooted to the ground, fighting down the part of her that wanted to go on screaming, wanted to run panic-wild back into the open. Fighting to stay with herself, not to let her fear win, was as desperate as riding Shantih over cross-country jumps, required the same energy.

106

"Breathe slowly," said Ken's voice in her head. Jinny grabbed it. Gulped in air and slowly breathed it out. Slowly breathed in and out, until her panic breath was calmed and controlled.

Jinny went down both passages. After a short distance they both ended in a blank stone wall. Both were completely empty.

Winding up the twine as she went, Jinny scuttled back along the tunnel. She came out into the cave. Before, it had seemed dark, now, compared to the tunnel, it was almost light.

Jinny unknotted the twine. Free from the claustrophobic passages, she was shaking with relief.

A movement halfway up the wall of the cave caught her eye. She glanced up. Outstretched on a ledge of rock the wolf was watching her. Jinny went numb with shock. She could only stand, staring back into the yellow eyes of the wolf. They seemed to blaze in the dimness, fixed and piercing and remote.

For minutes Jinny stood absolutely motionless. Her hands holding the torch and the twine stayed exactly where they had been when she first set eyes on the wolf. Very slowly, feeling and thought thawed back into Jinny – feelings of danger, real danger; feelings of fear and, just as real, the satisfaction of knowing that she had been right, a wolf had escaped from Bendarroch and it had been killing the sheep. Not Kelly. He was innocent as Jinny had always known he was.

The wolf stood up, shook itself and lay down again, its front legs outstretched, its head lifted, watching her.

"I've got to get past it," Jinny thought. "Got to get out of here."

She spreadeagled herself against the cave wall, pressing herself into the stone, inching her way along the wall on the opposite side to the wolf. As she came closer and closer to it every nerve in her body told her to run, to make a dash for it.

" 'You must never run from anything immortal'," said Ken's voice in her head, quoting from one of his favourite books. " 'Never run'."

When Jinny drew level with the wolf she could smell it,

and its smell was as terrifying as its gaunt, huge-boned head, the muscular bulk of its shoulders, the tight, steel-sinewed legs and knuckled paws.

The wolf turned its head slowly, following Jinny's progress, its ears tuned to her least sound. She was level with it and then past it. The cave opening was in front of her, the wolf behind her.

" 'Walk very slowly, magician'."

At the entrance to the cave Jinny stopped, glanced behind her she took a line to where Shantih waited, then, walking backwards, Jinny made her way towards her. When the cave mouth was only a black gap in the hillside, Jinny spun round and ran full tilt to Shantih.

With shaking hands, Jinny girthed on Shantih's saddle, pulled on her bridle, slung her rucksack over her shoulder, untied the halter rope and, holding rope and reins in her hands, flung herself on to Shantih's back and dug her heels into Shantih's sides. The Arab, catching Jinny's terror, reared into a gallop and Jinny didn't slow her down until they reached the standing stones – dark bulks in the mists that were beginning to wreath the moors.

When she reached home, Jinny left Shantih in her box and raced through the mist to the house.

"I've found it," she yelled to her mother as she burst into the kitchen. "I was right. There is a wolf."

Mrs. Manders stopped what she was doing and listened.

"What will you do now?" she asked when Jinny had finished.

"Got to phone Ralph Gilbert and tell him. He must come and catch it. Let the farmers know."

Jinny dashed to the hall. Fingers fumbling, she searched the directory for the Gilberts' number, and dialled.

"It's Jinny Manders," Jinny told the voice that answered. "I've got to speak to Ralph Gilbert. It's urgent."

The voice returned to say that Mr. Gilbert was not available, and put the phone down.

"No," said her mother firmly. "You cannot ride to Bendarroch tonight and that is final."

"Could Dad take me?"

"He's in town delivering pots. Should think this fog

will be too thick for him to go out again when he gets back."

Jinny phoned three more times in the next half-hour and each time the same voice informed her that Mr. Gilbert was not available. After that no one answered the phone.

Mike came in from school, alive with the adventure of riding Bramble home through the mists.

"Real pea soup at Glenbost. Much worse than it is here," he said. "Did you find Kelly?"

"Found the wolf," said Jinny and told him.

"What will you do now? Tell the farmers so they can shoot it?"

"No," cried Jinny. "They mustn't shoot it." She couldn't begin to tell Mike the strangeness of the wolf, the utter wildness of it.

"Then what?" asked Mike.

"I've got to tell Ralph Gilbert. He'll need to capture it. But he won't answer the phone." And Jinny went off to try again.

She let the phone ring for ten minutes but still no one answered. She banged the receiver down and instantly the phone rang. It was Mr. Manders to say that the fog was so bad he couldn't risk driving back to Finmory and was going to spend the night in Inverburgh.

"But I wanted you to drive me to Bendarroch," Jinny said and told her father about the wolf.

"Phone the police," suggested her father. "They would get through to the Gilberts."

"No," said Jinny coldly. "I don't want any more to do with the police."

"I'll be home tomorrow. I'll run you over then," promised her father.

Jinny made a non-committal noise and went to get her mother to speak to him.

The phone rang three more times that evening. The first call was Petra to say that although the school bus had set out it had been forced to turn back because of the fog.

The second call was from Moira Wilson, asking Jinny if she was going on Miss Tuke's winter trek. Jinny had utterly forgotten all about the Trekking Club meeting, could hardly think who Moira was.

"No," Jinny said. "No, I can't possibly come. I've got to save Kelly."

"What?" asked Moira. "Save who?"

But Jinny couldn't start and explain. "I am sorry," she said, "but I can't possibly come." And she put the phone down.

The third call was from Mr. Hendry. Jinny answered it but he wanted to speak to her father.

"He's stranded in Inverburgh," said Jinny. "Fogbound."

"Be taking the message yourself, then," instructed Mr. Hendry. "There's to be a shoot over the moors tomorrow."

"What do you mean, 'a shoot'?"

"We're for going out with the guns. There'll be the ten farmers and by the morn's night there'll be no grey brute on the hills killing our sheep. If your father has the notion to join us we'll be meeting in Mr. MacKenzie's yard at the back of nine."

Jinny sat down on the stairs to think. Before the farmers started their shoot tomorrow morning she had to let Ralph Gilbert know about his wolf. The farmers would listen to him. When he told them that it was his wolf that had escaped and was running wild on the hill they would call off the shoot and Kelly would be safe.

"First thing tomorrow morning," Jinny thought, "I'll ride to Bendarroch and make Ralph Gilbert listen to me."

CHAPTER TWELVE

Jinny woke to a world white with mist. Her clock said five past seven, and Jinny realised to her dismay that she had slept through the alarm. She had meant to be up at five. Still clumsy with sleep, she dressed and hurried out to Shantih, brought her in and gave her a feed. Back in the house, Jinny tried for the last time to phone Ralph Gilbert but whoever answered the phone replaced the receiver when they heard Jinny's voice.

Eating a fried egg sandwich and drinking coffee, Jinny still had no clear plan of action. She only knew that she should have been away by now, should have been half-way to Bendarroch.

"It's you," said her mother, coming into the kitchen.

"I'm riding to Bendarroch," Jinny told her between mouthfuls of sandwich. "I'll probably be away all day."

"You are beyond me," said her mother calmly. "Why won't you wait until Dad comes home?"

But Jinny hadn't time to listen. She pulled on her jacket, considered putting on her riding mack but decided against it. It was too stiff, too bulky. It would hold her back if she had to ride fast.

"Do try to be sensible," said Mrs. Manders.

"I always try," said Jinny, making no promises, and ran out of the house.

She took a dandy brush over Shantih and tacked her up, then led her out into a white world of mist.

Shantih plunged and fretted while Jinny mounted.

"On you go," said Jinny, sending her on at a trot down the lane to Mr. MacKenzie's.

Mist monsters loomed about them from every side. Trees, gigantic in the haze, appeared suddenly before them. A rusted milk churn, an abandoned sack, waited to pounce. Shantih shied violently, throwing herself from side to side of the lane in a zigzag of fear.

"Oh, stop it, Give over. There's nothing to be afraid of. It just looks different in the mist," Jinny said, sitting down hard and driving Shantih on with her seat and legs.

The wet mist in her face woke Jinny up, brought home to her how late she was. "Must be nearly nine o'clock," she thought. "I should have been at Bendarroch by now."

She heard a car creeping through the mist and knew from the sound that it was turning into Mr. MacKenzie's yard. The car stopped, doors were opened and banged shut, and men's voices, loud through the mist, reached Jinny. As she rode past the farm and out on to the road, Jinny caught stray scraps of conversation – assurances that the mist was clearing, that they would get the brute today, and Mr. MacKenzie asking them in for a dram and telling them that he had the wee idea where the dog would be hiding.

Jinny trotted up Bendarroch drive, jumped down from

Shantih and, holding her reins, went up the steps to the front door and pulled the heavy metal bell-pull. She waited, rehearsing in her head the words she was going to say, but no one came. Again she tugged desperately at the bell.

"Come on, come on," she thought. "I'm too late as it is. There's no time to waste." In her mind's eye she saw the farmers gathering in Mr. MacKenzie's yard – or had they started out already? While she was standing there were they crossing the moors, spread out in a line, each man carrying a gun. Kelly would be wet and cold after a night alone on the hills. Would he see them as friends and go running, wagging to meet them?

"Oh, come on," cried Jinny aloud as she pulled the bell for a third time.

She heard footsteps, and the door was opened by the housekeeper who had served their tea the day the Trekking Club visited the Arabs.

"I must speak to Mr. Gilbert," Jinny said. "It's urgent. He must see me."

The woman's blank, surprised face stared back at Jinny.

"He wouldn't speak to me on the phone but when he hears what I've got to tell him he'll wish he had. I *must* see him."

"What name shall I say?" asked the housekeeper stiffly.

"Jinny Manders, and tell him he *must* come at once."

The woman went away, leaving Jinny hanging on to Shantih, who was messing about at the end of her reins, half rearing and digging at the immaculate gravel.

"Mr. Gilbert does not wish to speak to you," the housekeeper said, repeating words she had been told to say. "If you go on annoying him in this way Lady Gilbert will report the matter to the police. You are to leave the estate immediately."

"Can't he understand I'm trying to help him?" Jinny's voice caught in her throat. If she couldn't see Ralph Gilbert what could she do now to save Kelly? Ride back and tell the farmers where the wolf was hiding? But Jinny didn't want the wolf to be shot either. She wanted them both to be saved. "It's urgent," she pleaded. "Oh, please understand."

112

The housekeeper shut the door in Jinny's face.

"He might be with the Arabs," Jinny thought. "Or with the wolves."

She threw herself back on to Shantih, and trotted round the side of the house. At the gates to the stable yard where she hesitated, but decided to go down to the wolves enclosure first.

Mist wreathed the black branches of the rhododendrons, making Shantih quicksilver to ride, as Jinny forced her on. The high wall loomed in front of them and Jinny cantered Shantih along the path by the side of it. To Jinny's relief the door in the wall stood slightly open. Men's voices reached her as she flung herself to the ground, pushed her way through the door, dragging Shantih behind her. Standing in front of the wolves' enclosure were Mr. Paton and Ralph Gilbert.

At the sight of the wolves Shantih reared up, balancing on her hindlegs, striking out with her forelegs, as she had been trained to do in the circus. The men shouted, sprang back out of range.

"What the devil are you doing here?" demanded Mr. Gilbert. "I've warned you to keep away from this place."

Hanging desperately on to Shantih, Jinny turned to face him. "I'm here because you wouldn't speak to me on the phone. I know where your wolf is, the one you've lost. I can take you to it."

"Wolf?" said Mr. Paton. "We have no wolves here. What nonsense are you talking?"

But Ralph Gilbert looked straight at Jinny. "Where?" he said, seeming to loom over her, his eyes staring from his haggard face.

"Past the standing stones," said Jinny. "I saw it in a cave there yesterday. You've got to come now. If you come they'll listen to you. You can stop them shooting it. And Kelly. When you tell them that it's your wolf that's been killing the sheep they'll stop thinking that it's Kelly. They'll believe you."

"We have dogs, cross-bred alsatians," insisted Mr. Paton in a last attempt to deny the fact of the wolves, but Ralph Gilbert ignored him.

"How did you find her?" he demanded. "My men have been searching the moors ever since she escaped."

"A farmer told me where to look, where an animal would hide if it were living on the moors." As Jinny spoke, she realised that Mr. MacKenzie or one of his sons would be out on the shoot. They would be sure to have told the other farmers about the caves. "The farmers are out on the moors *now*. They're having an organised shoot to get the animal that's been killing their sheep. They'll go to the caves, and if we don't stop them they'll shoot your wolf."

As she spoke Jinny realised for the first time that there was another way in which the wolf could be saved. They would not go on hunting for a wolf they did not believe in if they had shot Kelly.

"We've got to go *now*. We've got to stop them."

"Could we get to the caves in a Range Rover?" Ralph Gilbert asked.

"No," said Jinny. "It's too marshy. You'd be bogged down."

"Can your mare jump? How fit is she?"

"She's fit," said Jinny, "and she can jump."

"There's a quick way on to Finmory moors from here, but you have to be able to jump."

"Shantih can jump anything you can."

Ralph Gilbert paused, considering Jinny and Shantih with his black eyes.

"Come on," screamed Jinny. "Oh, hurry, hurry or we'll be too late."

"Wait here," ordered Ralph Gilbert as he ran past the enclosure and through the door.

Mr. Paton waited with Jinny, not speaking, and the wolves loped along the wire of their enclosure, watching them.

When Ralph Gilbert returned he was riding a steel grey Arab mare. Her skin glowed with the lustre of perfect health and fitness. She moved disdainful of the earth, a quivering, delicate, steel-hard beauty. Ralph Gilbert sat with a deep seat, not moving in the saddle when his horse, seeing Shantih, half reared and shied. His hands, light on the reins, absorbed and checked the movement, steadied

114

her and brought her closer to Jinny who was already mounted on Shantih.

"I have a tranquillizer gun with me," Ralph Gilbert said to Mr. Paton, patting a bulge in his jacket. "Take the Range Rover to Number Seven forestry gate. I'll meet you there whatever happens. And now," he said, turning to Jinny, his hard face taut, his menacing eyes fixed on her, "let's ride."

He led the way past the wolves' enclosure and along a broad path between shrub-planted banks. Jinny, riding behind him, felt Pony Clubbish in her crash cap and jodhpurs. The grey mare, clipped and hard with her expertly-pulled mane and banged tail, made Shantih seem like a rough pony by comparison.

They reached the boundary wall of the estate, rode along it until they came to iron gates similar to the main gates. Beside the gates there was a swinging wooden gate set in V-shaped fences, which allowed people to come in and out without having to open the gates.

"We can jump here," said Ralph Gilbert, and Jinny knew from his expression that he was testing her. "I'll go first."

He gathered his grey together, she tituped on the spot, took two quick strides and cleared the wooden gate. Shantih pulled to follow her and Jinny let her canter at the gate, felt her spring and soar and land far out in an effortless arc.

"Well done," said Ralph Gilbert coldly but Jinny knew he thought she was good enough to ride with him.

They cantered along the fostery track until they came to a narrow, metalled road.

"About a mile of this and then we take to the hills again," Ralph Gilbert told Jinny as he trotted beside her. "Now fill me in on this whole business."

Jinny told him how Kelly had been accused of sheep killing, how she had noticed that there had only been five wolves when she saw them the second time and she had thought that one had escaped and was on the moors, how Kelly had disappeared now and how he would be shot if they couldn't stop the farmers.

Jinny's words spurred her on. Shantih sensed her

115

urgency and increased her speed, the rhythmic beat of her trot pounding the road.

"When you lost the wolf why didn't you tell the police?" Jinny asked accusingly. "They would never have suspected Kelly if you'd told them."

"I couldn't risk telling them. The wolves are part of my experiments."

"Not shutting them up and putting wires in their heads and cutting bits of them up while they're still alive?" Jinny demanded in total disgust. As she spoke, Jinny knew that she had always felt there was something evil about Ralph Gilbert and his wolves. Who knew what went on behind the high, enclosing wall, or inside the buildings with their barred windows that had to be guarded by armed men?

Jinny felt suddenly sick. The fact that live animals were used for experiments was something she knew but never allowed herself to think about. She kept the knowledge securely battened down in the depths of her mind. She could not bear to face the fact that it was true. Even now she couldn't really believe that Ralph Gilbert could have anything to do with such cruelty.

"You don't do that sort of thing, do you?" she demanded again. Ralph Gilbert glanced back at her. Somewhere, Jinny had read that you saw a person's true face when they looked back at you over their shoulder. There was in Ralph Gilbert's backward glance a sly, secret satisfaction, a small boy absorbed in pulling the wings off a butterfly, a leering, secret cruelty.

"We turn off here," he shouted, and, making no attempt to answer Jinny's question, he turned his horse and popped her over a low hawthorn hedge. Before Jinny had time to realise what was happening, Shantih had followed him. Jinny was left behind, thumping down in the saddle, and she just managed to let the reins slip through her fingers and stop herself catching Shantih in the mouth.

Ralph Gilbert didn't hesitate. He had pushed his mare into a gallop and was racing up the hillside. Jinny galloped after him, the speed coursing through her, filling her with urgency. They must reach the caves before the farmers. Yet, as Jinny galloped, there was a heaviness in

116

her, a dread that already they might be too late; that already the shoot might be over and Kelly dead.

"I shouldn't have cared about the wolf," Jinny thought as she rode behind Ralph Gilbert up a straight way cut through the fungus of trees. "I should have gone to the police. I should have told Mr. MacKenzie where the wolf was hiding so that they could have shot it. If he is torturing them the wolf would be better dead. But I couldn't I couldn't have done it. Petra would have. Dolina would have. But I couldn't. I have to try to save both of them."

They came out of the pines and Ralph Gilbert turned to the right. There was just enough ground between the end of the forestry and the bare grey rock above it to allow them to find a pathway.

The going was rough, rock patched with soft peat and pine needles. Sawn-off pine branches littered the ground. Dry stone walls reached down to the trees, their fallen, scattered stones making them risky jumps. Shantih plunged and fought her way through the deep going. Twice, Jinny glimpsed vertical shards of pine trunks sticking up from the peat. If Shantih were to stake herself on one of them Jinny knew that she could be lamed for life.

By herself, Jinny would have trotted or walked, but Ralph Gilbert galloped relentlessly on in front of her. His grey Arab flew over the walls. She seemed free from gravity, galloping on invisible wings.

Jinny could feel Shantih tiring as she slipped and missed her footing more often. "His horse hasn't been ridden all the way from Finmory," Jinny thought, but she knew that Shantih couldn't possibly be as fit as a clipped, stabled horse.

As they galloped Jinny talked to Shantih, praising and encouraging her, telling her that they would save Kelly, that they would reach the wolf before the farmers.

They left the brooding darkness of the pines and rode across moorland completely new to Jinny. The folds and flow of the Finmory moors were so familiar to her that she felt strange riding on hills so similar yet different.

There was the sound of roaring water ahead of them. Shantih heard it and pricked her ears to listen. As they rode towards it, it grew into the crash and thunder of a

117

waterfall. The water came from grey rock high above them, a white streak of falling force; it flowed along the moorland then fell into a thunderous cascade of white water. Normally, the stretch of water between the two falls would have flowed smooth and deep, but now, after the recent heavy rain, it was as turbulent as the waterfalls.

Ralph Gilbert had stopped. His horse was shying and baulking, refusing to go near the rushing water. He turned as Jinny rode up to him.

"It's no use," he said. "They could never clear that today. We'll have to go back to the forestry roads."

Jinny stared at the rushing, crushing, headlong crash of the water. A horse jumping and not managing to reach the other side could be swept off its legs and carried to its death at the foot of the fall.

"If we turn back we will be too late," she said, the roar of the water almost drowning her voice. "We'd have no chance. We've got to jump it."

"Suicidal to risk it."

"But we must," insisted Jinny. Suddenly her patience snapped. "If you won't, I will," she said, her temper rising. "It's no use being afraid now."

Jinny glared at Ralph Gilbert, hating him, for it was all his fault; his fault that Kelly had been taken to the police station, branded as a sheep-killer and was being hounded over the moors. If his wolf hadn't escaped, none of this would have happened. The thought echoed in Jinny's mind, and before she could stop herself she had thought that none of it would have happened if Ken hadn't gone to Amsterdam. For a second the bleak misery of Ken's betrayal swamped over Jinny. "He wouldn't even come to the phone," she thought, tears behind her eyes, and shouted, "If you won't jump it I will."

"Now steady on," cautioned Ralph Gilbert. "If you're game we'll have a bash."

"Then get on with it," snapped Jinny.

Ralph Gilbert found the place where he normally jumped the water.

"See that rock," he said, pointing it out to Jinny. "Keep it on your left. Usually that gives you a sound landing, but Lord knows what it will be like today."

He took his mare back from the edge of the river, swung her round and rode her at it at a gallop. Within three strides of the water she stopped dead and reared up, terrified by the force of the river. Ralph Gilbert was almost thrown from her back but somehow he managed to stay in the saddle and calm her.

"It's impossible," he said when he had his horse under control again. "No horse would face that. We're wasting time. Better go back."

"I'll give you a lead," said Jinny, concentrating her mind on the courage with which Shantih had jumped Miss Tuke's cross-country course.

She rode Shantih to the water's edge. "It's for Kelly," she said. "You've got to jump it to save Kelly."

Shantih took in the size of the leap and Jinny felt her gather herself beneath her. Accepting the challenge, she mouthed at her bit, arched her neck and danced.

Jinny rode her away from the river, then turned and galloped her at the mad, exploding froth. There was no doubt in Jinny. She knew that Shantih would take her to the other side.

Shantih leapt the water as if she were jumping a five-barred gate. She soared over it. For a split moment Jinny was held in an entire world of white water. Above her was the fall down the rock face, beneath her the river, and below, the resonant, groaning roar of the waterfall.

Ralph Gilbert jumped close behind her. His grey hesitated, torn between fear of the river and fear of being left behind, then she flung herself across, landing safely on the other side.

From somewhere in the vastness of the moors there was the unmistakable whining crack of a gun being fired.

"Come on," cried Jinny. "We haven't any time."

With the sound of the bullet had come the imagined sight of Kelly lying dead on the heather.

CHAPTER THIRTEEN

Quite suddenly, the standing stones were there, black teeth in the moorland's empty mouth. Jinny, used to approaching them from the other direction, was taken by surprise. Despite the delay at the waterfall they had reached the stones in a faster time than Jinny would have thought possible.

They galloped on until they were standing in the stone circle.

"Give them a breather," said Ralph Gilbert, dismounting.

"We haven't time," said Jinny, but she jumped to the ground and turned Shantih's head into the breeze. Jinny had always thought of herself as riding fast over the moors but Ralph Gilbert had set his grey into a steady gallop and kept her at that speed, not checking her for walls or marsh. They had galloped without pause from the waterfall to the stones.

Jinny stared round about her, eyes sharp, looking for the farmers. She looked behind her first, back towards Finmory. There was no sign of them. The cold certainly clutched at Jinny that one shot had been enough. They had shot Kelly and gone back to Mr. MacKenzie's for whisky and talk.

"It's up to you now," said Ralph Gilbert. "You know the way from here."

"The caves are over there," Jinny said, searching for the rowans.

Banners of mist still covered the moors. Gathering and flowing, in minutes covering over landmarks and in minutes exposing them.

"There," said Jinny, pointing, as she made out the shapes of the rowans, barely visible through the mists.

There was something else close to the trees. A dark shape moving away from them. Tantalizingly, the mist breathed about it, so that Jinny couldn't see it clearly.

"What's that?" she said. As she spoke she saw another figure in line with the first, and then another. They were men walking in line; men carrying guns.

"It's them. There. The shoot. They're in front of us."

Ralph Gilbert looked through the mist to where Jinny was pointing and saw them too.

"If they reach the wolf first they'll shoot her and the whole place will be alive with gossip," he said, already jumping back on to his horse.

Jinny hardly had time to spring on to Shantih before Ralph Gilbert was galloping off. Side by side, the Arabs galloped across the flat land. The mists made it difficult to judge distances. One minute it seemed that they had almost reached the rowans, the next as if they were as far away from them as ever.

Jinny had lost all sense of time or place. She seemed to have been galloping Shantih for days. The stone walls they had jumped were blurred in her mind, the moorland falling away beneath the hooves of their horses might have been a backcloth on a moving stage where the horses galloped endlessly only to stand still.

"Don't stop," Ralph Gilbert warned her when they had passed the rowans. "Ride straight through them. Don't let them turn you back."

Jinny saw a farmer to her right. He was a dark shape looming through the mist. He had heard the horses and was looking round for them. He saw Jinny and came running, boot-footed, towards her. Jinny swung Shantih away from him, heard Ralph Gilbert shout from in front of her, "To your left. Look out to your left!"

Jinny looked round quickly and saw Mr. Hendry almost at her side, his arm outstretched to grasp Shantih's bridle.

"What are you at now?" he shouted at her.

The sudden voice scared Shantih. She plunged forward and let fly with both hind feet, narrowly missing the farmer.

They were through the line of the shoot and the caves lay in front of them. From their own courage the Arabs seemed to find a final burst of speed.

"We're there. We've made it," Jinny thought as the dark mouths of the caves became visible.

Ralph Gilbert demanded the last ounce of speed from his grey. "Hope she's still here. All this noise may have scared her away," he shouted.

Jinny hadn't thought of it. She had imagined that the wolf must be in the cave, waiting for them, but of course it might not be there now.

Ralph Gilbert brought his horse to a halt a little way from the caves.

"Where exactly did you see her?"

"That one. The largest opening," replied Jinny, dropping from Shantih. Her legs were chewed elastic and she clung to the saddle to stop herself collapsing. She had brought Ralph Gilbert to the wolf, but now she knew what his animals were used for she only wished that the wolf could have found its way further north and lived free in the mountains.

Ralph Gilbert handed Jinny his reins. "Wait here," he said, taking his tranquilliser gun from an inside pocket he began to walk towards the caves.

The wolf, a grey shadow, came to the cave mouth. Instantly Ralph Gilbert took aim and fired.

"No! No!" Jinny screamed as the wolf leapt into the air and then slumped to the ground. It struggled to rise, fell back and lay still.

"Only dope," Ralph Gilbert shouted to Jinny. "That lot should keep it quiet for four or five hours."

"And now for the farmers," he added, turning from the wolf to face the dark shapes of men running towards them through the mist. "This will soon settle them." Ralph Gilbert took a roll of twenty-pound notes from his pocket.

The farmers came closer. They were big men, broad-shouldered and hardy, who had lived all their lives on hill farms. Suddenly Jinny saw that one of them was wearing a blue uniform, and she recognised the policeman from Ardtallon.

Ralph Gilbert saw him at the same time as Jinny and instantly his whole expression changed. He had been waiting for the farmers, smooth and arrogant, money in his hand to buy them off, but now he looked scared. For a moment Jinny thought he was going to spring back on to his horse and try to escape, but he hesitated and was too late.

"Tell them that there was only one wolf at Bendarroch. Tell them you only saw one wolf," he muttered desperately to Jinny. "I'll pay you what you like. Anything you like but tell them this was the only wolf you saw."

"What?" demanded Jinny, but before Ralph Gilbert had time to explain the policeman had reached them.

"Mr. Gilbert," he said. "Fancy that we should be meeting here on the moors like this. And yourself the very one I'm looking for."

"I can't think why you should be looking for me," blustered Ralph Gilbert. "I don't think you even know who I am."

"That I do, for it's the wee bit of checking up that I've been doing on you, Mr. Gilbert, and it's yourself I'm wanting and no mistake."

"What do you mean by that?"

"I mean what I'll be telling you in a minute, but first I've to thank the lassie here for putting me on your trail. She was so sure that it was the wolves she'd seen at Bendarroch she put the doubt into my own mind, and I did the wee research. I'm thinking you'll be the same Ralph Gilbert who was convicted three years ago in Dorset for carrying out illegal experiments on the poor beasts, and it's serious trouble you'll be in this time if you've been at your cruelties again."

"What proof have you?" Ralph Gilbert demanded, his voice loud and confident, his face white. "This is the wolf the girl saw. It's a pet wolf, the only one I have. Ask the girl to tell you herself." He swung round on Jinny. "Tell him," he commanded.

Jinny gulped. Ralph Gilbert's cold eyes stared piercingly at her. His lips peeled back from sharp teeth and his flat cheeks were clamped into his jaws.

"There's six wolves," Jinny said loudly. "This one and five more at Bendarroch."

Ralph Gilbert swore at Jinny. He lunged forward and grabbed her arm but instantly the policeman had pushed him back.

"No need to involve the lassie. There's police at Ben-

123

darroch now. If you have any more animals they'll find them."

"I shouldn't think Lady Gilbert will allow them in."

"I'm thinking even her Ladyship will be taking heed of a search warrant. She did her best to have the whole matter covered up last time. She didn't manage it then and she won't manage it now," said the policeman calmly.

"If you can't find them," Jinny said, "they're hidden away behind a wall beyond the rhododendron scrubberies."

"I'm thinking the police dogs will have no trouble smelling them out," the policeman assured her. "And now, Mr. Gilbert, shall we be getting ourselves back to Bendarroch? You'll have your arrangements made, I'm thinking."

Suddenly Ralph Gilbert admitted that Mr. Paton was waiting for him in the Range Rover.

"Then we'll be going down to meet him," said the policeman. "I know the way fine."

The farmers tied the wolf's legs and muzzle and one of the young men slung it over his shoulders.

"Oh, be careful," cried Jinny, as the wolf's head lolled down the man's back. "You won't shoot them, will you?" she pleaded anxiously.

"We will not," said the policeman. "They'll all be for the safari park and a happier life they'll be having there than they'd ever known with him."

Jinny stood watching as the three men, Ralph Gilbert leading his horse, made their way over the moor. She would never see the wolf again. She remembered the moment in the cave when they had been so close to one another and tears pricked in Jinny's eyes. "It's all a mess," she thought bitterly. "A rotten mess." Then she scrubbed at her eyes with clenched fists. There was nothing she could do to change things, she couldn't stop humans torturing animals, not just now, anyway. She had to find Kelly.

Jinny turned to the group of farmers who were still standing about, talking.

"Now that you know it wasn't Kelly who was killing your sheep, you can tell me if you've seen him," she said.

"We're owing you the apology for putting the black

name on your dog," Mr. Hendry said. "You can see how the mistake happened."

"If you'd listened to me it wouldn't have happened," said Jinny. "You all thought I was making up the story about the wolf, just to shield Kelly. Well, I wasn't."

"We were wrong," said Mr. Hendry. "You have our apologies."

"What good would that have been if you'd shot Kelly the way you wanted to? He'd have been dead now. What good would your apologies have done then?"

Jinny scowled at the farmers, refusing to give in and make polite that's-all-right-then noises.

"And where is Kelly now?" she demanded.

"You'd better be telling her," said Ewan MacKenzie.

"What?" cried Jinny. "Better tell me what?"

She was leaning against Shantih, holding on to her as the only safe thing in this violence of men and guns.

The farmers glanced guiltily at each other. Mr. Hendry spoke. "We'd the sight of the dog earlier this morning and we took a wee shot at him, thinking he was the killer, you understand."

Clinging to Shantih, Jinny waited for them to tell her that Kelly was dead. It was what they had wanted and now they had managed it.

"We think we hit him but he got away from us."

"You mean he's on the moor now, wounded?"

"Don't you be upsetting yourself. It may be only the scratch he'll have. We'll be looking out for him on our way back."

"Bloody killers," swore Jinny. "You and your guns."

"Now, now, there'll be no call for such language," said one of the men as they began to move away.

"We'll keep the look-out for him," another called back.

"Kelly," Jinny called as she rode back over the moors. "Kelly." But there was no trace or sight of the dog.

"We'll go home," she decided when they reached the stones. "I'll need to get the others to help me search for him. I'll never find him by myself. And you've done enough for one day," she told Shantih.

As Jinny rode towards Finmory she relived the ride from Bendarroch to the caves. "You were the best horse," she told Shantih proudly. "For all her polish his horse was afraid to jump. But you weren't."

Finmory came into sight and Jinny quickened her pace, asking Shantih to trot. Although she had called Kelly as she rode, no grey, shaggy dog had come bursting through the heather. "He could be lying wounded, hearing me and not able to come to me," Jinny thought desperately. "Oh, Kelly! Kelly!"

When Jinny had watered and fed Shantih she leant against the box wall, waiting for her horse to finish eating. She was tired, tired enough to lie down where she was and fall asleep, but she couldn't. She had to tell her family what had happened. Make them come out on to the moors with her and search for Kelly. They had to find him before it got dark, had to get him to the vet if he was wounded.

"Hi," said Ken, opening the door, walking into the box. "How's things?"

Jinny stared in total disbelief. It couldn't be. But it was.

"Ken!" she cried. "Ken!"

"I've come home," Ken said, looking exactly the same as when she had last seen him at the station. "I've had too much."

"But you wouldn't even come to the phone."

"Bob never told me. He knew I'd had enough but he wanted me to stay; knew I'd leave if he told me about Kelly. Only last night that I heard. So I split. It wasn't the place for me. Arty crafty. Tied on with string. I knew from the day I got there but I hadn't the guts to admit it to myself."

"You mean you're back to stay?" shouted Jinny.

"I am," said Ken.

"Oh joy," cried Jinny, the whole world diamonds and rainbows. Life could go on again now that Ken was back. "Where's Kelly?"

"On the moors," said Jinny. "The farmers shot at him."

Ken held out his hand to her. "Let's find him," he said.

They ran together up the track to the hillside. Ken called his dog, his voice flying over the moors.

"Kelly. Kelly."

The dog came over the skyline at them. Bounding through the bracken, tongue lolling and tail a blurr of happiness. He threw himself at Ken, crying and yelping his delight as he leapt about him. Ken knelt down and Kelly flung his paws round Ken's neck – dog over the moon to have his master back again.

When Kelly's first ecstatic welcome had worn itself out they examined him to see if he had been hurt but they could find nothing.

Going back to Finmory, Jinny told Ken all that had happened.

"Heavy," said Ken. "I should have come back when I knew it was no use but my pig head made me stay."

"You're back now."

"Homeland," said Ken.

Ken and Kelly went into the kitchen together, and, waiting outside, Jinny could hear the excited voices of her mother and father welcoming him. She went down to the stable to turn Shantih out. Soon she would be coming in at night, standing in deep straw, warm against the winter gales; Bramble in his stall beside her.

As Jinny went into her box, Shantih whinnied gently, rubbed her head against Jinny's arm and walked companionably by Jinny's side down to the field.

"Horse," said Jinny, turning her loose. "Dear, dear horse. I love you best of all."

Jinny stood for a moment watching Shantih roll, then she walked slowly back to the house. Maybe happiness was an immortal thing too, perhaps you shouldn't run to it. "Walk slowly magician".

As she walked slowly, happiness brimmed over in Jinny. "Thank you, thank you," she said aloud and then forgetting all about walking slowly she ran full tilt up the garden path, taking great leaps into the air, arms wide, hair flying, for Kelly was safe and Ken had come home.

Armada